DON'T SMOTHER YOUR MOTHER

I0537429

By

Susan L. Paré

This book is a work of fiction. Names, characters, places, and incidents are either a product of the author's imagination or are used fictionally. Any resemblance to actual persons, living or dead, or the actual events or locales is entirely coincidental.

Cover designed by: Susan L. Pare'

ISBN-13:978-0-9966195-1-6

www.susanlpare.com

DEDICATION

To Joyce Shoup, my friend and probably my biggest fan. She constantly builds me up and makes me think I just might know what I'm doing. Thanks, Joyce, for your love and friendship.

MORE BY THIS AUTHOR

The Finger

The Twisted Tree Triangle

The Box House

The Proof is in the Pudding

Blueberries and Bears and My Brother's Shoes

Red, White, and Blue (A Short Story)

She Never Stopped Talking

Red

The House on Ludington Street

What's Behind the Screen Door?

The Mayor's Son

Willerton Woods

Cowtown (Unavailable)

Floating Face Down
A Sheriff "Cowboy" Berkson Mystery Novel – Book
Three

Let's Play Autopsy

A Bad Week In Hollister
A Sheriff "Cowboy" Berkson Mystery Novel – Book Two

Crossing Sydney

Contents

"ALL IS NEVER ENOUGH"

Prologue

1992, Hollister, Missouri

"Get away from him," Melissa screamed. "I swear to god if you hit him one more time, I'll kill you."

"Put that gun down, Missy, or you'll be next."

"I mean it. I'll fucking kill you."

Joe raised the belt over his head and brought it down hard, hitting the boy on his little bleeding back. The little boy cried out and Melissa screamed, "No!" She raised the .45, fired, and blew off a chunk of Joe's right ear.

"You bitch! You shot me," he yelled.

"Leave right now, Joe. While you can still walk."

"I'm gonna beat the living crap out of you," he yelled at her. "Then, I'm gonna beat this sissy boy of yours again, while I make you watch. Got that, bitch?"

Joe took a menacing step towards her, paying no attention to the blood dripping from his injured ear onto his shirt. Melissa backed away, still aiming the gun at him.

"I figure I can kill you right where you stand," she said, "Or, I can shoot your pecker off. Which do you prefer?"

As Joe started to take another step towards her, she fired a shot into the floor next to his boot.

"Last chance, Joe. Walk out that door right now and don't ever show your face around here again."

"And, if I don't?"

"Then you're a dead man."

"Take it easy. I'm going," he said

She kept the gun aimed at him as he walked to the front door, opened it, and turned back towards her.

"I'll be back," he told her, as he walked out the door. "Believe me. When you least expect it, I'm gonna show up."

"Get out. Now. Before I change my mind," Melissa screamed.

She locked the door and ran to her son. She picked him up, put him on her lap, and held him.

"Don't cry, Johnnie. Mama's here. Everything is going to be okay. Your daddy isn't going to hurt you again. I'll take care of you. You're my big boy."

Through his sobs, the little boy tried to smile at her. "I'm your big John, right, mama."

"That's right, sweetheart," Melissa said, tears rolling down her cheeks. "You'll always be my Big John."

Sheriff Dudley and his deputy, Officer Jason 'Cowboy' Berkson, were sitting on the couch talking to Melissa.

"I need to get John to the hospital," she said. "Can you take us? Joe took the car and I don't have a way to get there. Someone has to look after the baby and Bobby."

"Cowboy," the sheriff said. "You stay here with the kids while I take Melissa and her boy to the hospital."

"You want me to watch a baby?" he replied. "I don't know nothing about watching a baby."

"Now's as good a time as ever to learn," said the sheriff to his deputy. "And, if that no-good son of a bitch shows up again—shoot him.

"Will do,"

"Come on, Melissa. Let's get that boy of yours to the hospital," said the sheriff.

"Are you gonna arrest Joe?" she asked him.

"I will if I find him. But I'll bet you the tail off a rattlesnake he's long gone," the sheriff replied.

One

2010, Hollister, Missouri

"If I have to tell you one more time that we do not- let me repeat that- we do not - live in a trailer, I'm going to kick your butts up one street and down the other. This is not a trailer. This is a mobile home. Trailers have wheels. We do not."

The recipients of this outburst were her three sons who were trying hard not to laugh. Big John finally let loose with a big snort, cracking up his two brothers.

"What difference does it make, mama?" asked Bobby, while trying to keep a straight face. "It would be a trailer if we put the wheels back on it, right? What's bugging you anyway?"

"My daddy thinks we live in a nice house down here in Hollister. If some day you boys slip up and say trailer instead of house, he's gonna know I've been exaggerating my status here all these years."

"Just what do you think the chances are that we're gonna be talking to him more than our once-a-year Christmas call? We only talk to him then because you make sure we thank him for the five dollars he sends us," said Big John.

"You're just lucky to get that. It used to be a dollar. I don't get anything from him. He hasn't given me a lick since

I left home at eighteen. He's one tight-fisted old man,"

"Then why even worry about it?' asked Bobby.

"Why? I'll tell you why. That old fart has some money stuck away some place. I just know it and I plan to be in that Will of his when he finally kicks the bucket. Yes, sir. If I stay on his good side, I'll be rich someday. You just watch and see."

"So, watcha gonna do if he decides to stop by and visit us someday? Hide out under the bed and not answer the door?" asked her youngest son, Tom.

"You think you're funny, don't you? Well, I can tell you three smart asses, that's never gonna happen. He only leaves home twice a year. One, when he travels to Florida for the winters, and, two, when he goes fishing in Canada in June. We're just plain out of his way and not convenient. No worries there, boys."

"Well, Mama, I hope your right 'cause he'd cut you off for sure if he saw the dump we're living in," said Tom.

"Well, Tom, if you think you live in a dump, why don't you get a job and start contributing, so we can move? This dump seems to be good enough for you to live in, rent-free."

Laughing, Big John added, "I'm sure not gonna worry about it. Grandpa is going to outlive you and Mary Ellen. You'll never see a penny of his money, Mom, so best quit dreaming about it."

"You know I do the best I can with little help from any of

you three smart asses," she said and started to cry.

"Oh, crap," said Bobby, "Here comes the waterworks. Come on, guys. Let's go get a beer."

Melissa watched as her three sons walked out the door. What the hell, she thought. They could have asked me. I would have liked a beer.

Melissa had married their dad, Fat Joe, when she was just out of high school. People didn't call him Fat Joe back then, but all that beer drinking had turned him into a fat slob.

Kicking Joe out and divorcing him was the best thing I ever did, she thought. At least he's not around to spend all that money I'll get when daddy dies. He'd just blow it on booze and gambling and we'd be broke in no time. That no-good son of a bitch never did know how to handle money. If he was down to his last quarter, he'd buy a gumball from a gumball machine. Couldn't keep a penny in his pockets just like he couldn't keep his pecker in his pants.

Melissa decided to give her father a call and see how he was doing. She figured out of sight - out of mind - and she sure didn't want that to happen.

She picked up the phone and called her father.

"Samuel Clinton. State your business and if you're selling, I'm not buying."

"Hi, Daddy, it's me, Melissa. How you doing?"

"Melissa, darlin', is something wrong?"

"No, Daddy, I just thought I'd call and say hi and see how you're feeling. Haven't talked to you since Christmas. Time does fly by, doesn't it?"

"Well, it sure as hell does. What do you think it's gonna do? Stand still. I'm not lending today, so I hope you're not looking for money."

"Of course not, Daddy. I just wanted to say hi and see how you are."

"I'm absolutely fine. You realize that you could write me a letter for a lot less than this phone call is costing you. You're just wasting your money if you haven't got anything important to say to me."

"I'm sorry, Daddy. I just wanted to hear your voice. I miss you."

"Well, then, you shouldn't have moved away. If you had stayed here where you belonged, you wouldn't have to make these expensive phone calls. You could just come over and visit me."

"Daddy, that was over twenty years ago. Can't you just get over it?"

"At least your sister stayed here. At least I have one daughter that takes care of me now that your mother's gone."

"I know. Mary Ellen is your good daughter. I have to go, Daddy. Take care of yourself."

"Damn him," she said, so pissed off she threw the phone, which went flying across the kitchen, hit the refrigerator, and broke into pieces. A large plastic piece boomeranged back and hit her on her forehead. She let out a yelp, took a step backward, tripped over her own feet, and landed hard on her butt. "Son of a bitch, that hurt," she said as she stood up. She touched her forehead with her fingertip, looked at it, and saw blood.

"Shit," she said. "I just can't win for losing."

Two

2015, Hollister Missouri

"But I don't want to move out. I like it here," whined Tom.

"Of course, you do. Who wouldn't like living here? You've never paid rent, you eat free, and you've never done one thing around here to help. You're a bum. You can't keep a job more than a couple of months. Now, you have the nerve to ask me if your pregnant girlfriend can live with us. I don't think so."

"Mom, please. We don't have any other place to go. Her parents won't let us live with them. What are we supposed to do?"

"I'll tell you what you should have done. Kept it in your pants, that's what. You just better find a place to live, young man, 'cause you aren't bringing that skank here. How do you even know it's your kid?"

"Mom, please. I'll start paying rent."

"Just where do you think you're gonna sleep? You already share a room with Bobby and you sure as hell ain't getting my room."

"Why can't Bobby and Big John share a room?"

"You know what? If you can get Big John to give up his room, then I'll say yes. I'll give you one month. If it doesn't work out, then you and your no-good girlfriend are out of here," Melissa said.

"I'll tell Molly to pack her stuff," said Tom.

"The hell you will. You gotta talk to Big John first and I already know that's not gonna fly. There's no way he's gonna give up his room for your sorry ass. And, even if you get lucky and he says yes, you're still going have to start paying rent - up front - before she can move in."

"How much are you talking about?" said Tom.

"Well, let's see. You, Molly, and a baby. I figure a thousand a month. And, you buy your own groceries. No more eating my food. You wanna act like a big man and get some girl pregnant, then you gonna pay the price. Yep, I figure a couple grand up front. First month's rent and security deposit. And, the first time you miss a payment, you're out of here,"

"For one dumb fucking bedroom? You gotta be nuts. I can rent a place cheaper than that."

"Exactly. So, why don't you do that and get the hell out of my house? You and your brothers have been sponging off of me for years now and it's time for all of you to just get the hell out."

"Mom, please."

"No."

The room became so quiet you could hear a pin drop. Tom and Melissa had been sitting at the kitchen table for over an hour, arguing. There was nothing left to say.

Tom got up, went to the refrigerator, and took out a beer.

"Just what do you think you're doing?" Melissa asked.

"I'm gonna have a beer," Tom replied.

"It will cost you two dollars. Either hand over the money or put the beer back."

"Now I have to pay for a stinking beer?"

"That's the new rules. Nothing is free around here anymore."

Tom reached into his pocket, pulled out a five-dollar bill, and threw it at his mother.

"Put the beer back. I don't want your money." Melissa said.

Tom stood with the beer in his hand, glaring at her.

"You are one fucking bitch," he said and threw the bottle of beer at her.

She ducked in time for the bottle to miss her, but it hit the refrigerator, breaking into pieces. A good-sized piece of glass ricocheted off the frig and hit Melissa in the face, cutting her cheek.

"Son of a bitch," she said. "I gotta get rid of that refrigerator before it kills me."

Melissa sat in the emergency room, waiting to be stitched up, and thought about her sorry life. She was forty-five years old with three grown sons still living at home. She barely made ends meet and her sons didn't do much to help.

She had been waitressing for over twenty years. Living in Hollister did have some advantages, as it was close to Branson. Her waitressing job there paid good money during the busy season. It was during the winter months she got behind in her bills. I could save enough money to get through those tough months if I didn't have to keep feeding those boys, she thought to herself. It's definitely time to lay down the law. This crap with Tom is the last straw.

"Melissa," the nurse called, startling her back to reality. "The doctor will see you now."

Melissa called her sons as soon as she got home and informed them that a family meeting was to take place at seven o'clock. Attendance was mandatory, no excuses, and they had better be sure they showed up.

To her utter amazement, all her boys had listened to her and, at seven o'clock, they were sitting in the living room. It was no surprise, however, that they all had big goofy smiles on their faces. Everything was always a joke to them.

"Big John, Bobby, Tom – you know I love you all to pieces. There is nothing I wouldn't do for you. I think I have shown..." she started to say.

Big John interrupted her and said, "What's this all about, mom? I got plans and need to be out of here in half an hour. Can you just cut to the chase, please?"

"I'm getting there," Melissa yelled at him. "Can't you just be quiet for one minute and let me finish?"

"Sorry," Big John said, and added, "What the hell happened to your face?"

"Never mind about my face. The bottom line is this. Today Tom asked me if he could take over your room, Big John. He wants to bring his pregnant girlfriend here to live with us. Your brother, who has never contributed one thing around here, had the nerve to..."

"Well, I tried to pay you for a beer today but you wouldn't take it," said Tom.

Ignoring his smart remark, Melissa continued. "Bobby, you're eating me out of house and home. Just look at the size of you. You're getting fatter every day and I'm getting poorer every day just trying to feed you."

"Big John, at least you help out, but you're twenty-seven years old. It is time for you to find your own place to live. All of you need to find your own places. I'm not doing this anymore. I'm going to be fair about it. You have three months to find a place to live and vacate my premises. I'm tired boys. I'm tired of supporting three grown men and it ends now."

"I offered to pay rent and you turned me down," said Tom.

"You are not bringing a pregnant girl into this house, Tom. We already had this discussion, so forget it."

"Three months isn't a very long time, Mom," said Bobby. "I'll have to save up some money for first and last month's rent. Maybe you could give me six months. That would work better for me."

"If you want to be fair, then I should be able to stay another four years. Big John's lived here four years longer than I have. I should be able to stay as long as he did," said Tom.

"Then I should be able to stay another two years," Bobby commented.

"Three months is it," Melissa replied. "Maybe you three should find a place together. Then you'd only have one-third of the cost. Maybe you should talk about that."

"I'm sure as hell not living with those two pigs," said Big John.

"Well, we don't want to live with you either," said Bobby. "Tom, you want to get a place with me? I don't care if Molly moves in with us. It'll be fun living together."

"You know, Bobby, you'll wind up paying for everything. I'd be surprised if you see one dime from Tom," said Melissa.

"He's got three months to come up with his share," said Bobby.

"Good. It's settled," said Melissa. "I just can't wait to see how much fun you two will be having in a few months listening to a wailing baby, while you're trying to sleep.

Three

Melissa, Bobby, and Tom were sitting at the kitchen table, eating dinner "You know you only have a few weeks before you have to move," Melissa reminded them. "Have you boys found a place to live yet?"

"We're working on it, mama," said Bobby. "A friend of mine knows a guy who thinks his father might rent out an apartment he has over his garage. It's real cheap, too. He's out of town right now, but we'll know as soon as he comes back."

"Just when will that be?" inquired Melissa.

Before he could answer, the phone rang. Tom tilted his chair back and reached behind him to grab the phone. He misjudged the distance, leaned back too far, making the chair tip backward, spilling him onto the floor.

"Bobby, get that will you?" Melissa said. "I swear that boy is as useless as they get. Will someone answer that damn phone?"

Bobby got out of his chair, stepped over Tom who was still on the floor, and answered the phone.

"Hello. Yes, this is the Johnsons. Who? Yes, she's here. Who's calling? Oh, hi, Aunt Mary Ellen. How're you? That's nice. Sure, just a minute."

"It's Mary Ellen, Mom. She wants to talk to you," said Bobby.

"Really, Bobby? Like I didn't hear you talking. Give me

that phone," said Melissa, as Bobby handed her the phone.

"Hi, Mary Ellen. What's up? What? Slow down. What happened to daddy? Oh, my God, that's terrible. When did it happen? A week ago? Why are you just calling me now? What do you mean I should take it easy? Our daddy had an accident and I don't hear about it for a week."

Bobby and Tom watched as their mother talked. Obviously, something bad had happened, but their mother was smiling.

"Of course, I'm coming up," said Melissa. "I don't know about the boys, but I'll be there as soon as I can make arrangements. How long do they think he has? Oh, Mary Ellen, how horrible. I'll call you as soon as I know when I'll be leaving. No, I'm not flying. We'll drive up. I can't afford to fly. Besides, if I drive, we can all come."

Melissa finished her conversation with Mary Ellen and said goodbye. "Sit down, boys. I have bad news. It's about your grandpa."

"We heard," said Tom, still on the floor.

"Will you get up? Good lord, you drive me crazy. Grandpa's in a coma and they don't expect him to come out of it. The doctors told Mary Ellen that he probably won't last a week. We need to get going. Call Big John and tell him to get home. We have to pack."

"What's wrong with you?" said Bobby.

"What? Nothing. Why?"

"I just don't know if I've ever seen you look so happy."

Samuel Clinton died fifteen minutes before Melissa and her family arrived at the hospital.

When Melissa and her boys walked into the room, Mary Ellen and her husband, Peter, were sitting next to her father's bed. Mary Ellen was holding her father's hand and tears were pouring down her cheeks. When she saw Melissa, she jumped up, ran over to her, and hugged her.

"Oh, Melissa, daddy's gone. He died a few minutes ago. What am I going to do without daddy? I have no one now," she said.

Hearing that comment, Peter's head jerked up. "What am I?" he said. "Canned meat?"

"Well, of course, I still have you. You know what I meant, Peter. It's just that with both my mama and daddy gone, I'm an orphan."

"Well, maybe we can find someone to adopt you. For crying out loud, Mary Ellen, grow up. You're thirty-five years old and you still act like you're ten."

"My daddy just died and you dare talk to me like this? You never liked daddy. You're probably glad he's dead."

"Mary Ellen. Nobody liked your father," said Peter.

Melissa watched as her sister and brother-in-law carried on, thinking that some things never change. They had been fighting the last time she had seen them and they were fighting now. I wonder if they're ever nice to each other, she thought to herself.

"Stop it," Melissa said. "I didn't drive all the way up here from Missouri to hear you two fight. Save it for when I'm gone."

"So, Mary Ellen" she continued, "Have you made any funeral arrangements yet?"

"He just fucking died," said Mary Ellen. "Of course, I haven't made any arrangements. By the way, what happened to your face?"

"I got cut. Well, I'm going over to the house. Will you be here much longer?" asked Melissa.

"Aren't you even going to say goodbye to daddy? You're just going to walk out without saying goodbye?"

"Of course, I'm going to say goodbye. Actually, I'd like a few minutes alone with him. Would you and Peter give me a few minutes? Boys, you, too. Out."

Melissa sat down in a chair next to the bed and looked at her father. She glanced at the door and saw her sister watching her through the window. She took her father's hand and immediately let go. The old bastard felt weird. Just what was she supposed to say to him? He was dead.

Sister still watching? Yep, there she is.

"Daddy, I guess I'm supposed to say goodbye to you. I didn't see you much lately, but I guess I'll still miss you a little. Mary Ellen is sad enough for both of us. She's still crying out there in the hall. I guess I should be crying, too, now that you're dead, but Peter's right. Nobody really liked you. Not even mother. You were a cold man and now you're a dead cold man. I.... What the fuck?"

"Mary Ellen, get in here. Now!"

Mary Ellen, who was still watching her through the door, came running in yelling, "What's the matter? What are you yelling about?"

"Daddy moved. I swear he moved. I don't think he's dead."

Mary Ellen looked at her sister as if she had lost all her marbles. "What the hell are you talking about? Of course, he's dead."

"He moved. He took a breath. I saw it. Call the doctor."

"Mary Ellen laughed. "You dummy. That's just air leaving his lungs. Believe me, he's dead."

"Well, it's not funny. It scared me. I didn't know that happens. Okay, I've said my goodbyes. I'm heading over to the house. Why don't you come over when you're done here?" Melissa said.

"Just like always, I'm left to clean up the mess. Just leave. I'll talk to you later."

"We just drove eight hours to get here and I'm tired. Just call me later," said Melissa.

Four

Melissa and her three sons walked out of the hospital and piled back into her car. The short drive to Paw Paw from Mendota would take about fifteen or twenty minutes. From there, it was another five to reach her daddy's property, which was on the outskirts of town. Her father quit farming years ago, but he still owned the land, most of which he leased to neighboring farmers.

"How did Grandpa lose his arm?" asked Big John. "I think you told us once, but I forgot."

"You know, Big John, that's a real interesting question. He had an accident a long time ago," answered Melissa.

"Obviously, he had some kind of an accident," said Big John, "But, what happened?"

"It was raining and he was driving his tractor up that big old hill out back of the barn when a horse came out of nowhere. It was running right at him, just like it was blind or something. He pulled the tractor to the left to avoid hitting the horse and the tractor tipped over. He flew off and landed hard on the muddy ground, right in front of the panicked horse. The horse reared up and when it came down, one of its hoofs landed on your grandpa's arm, breaking a couple of bones," said Melissa.

"Couldn't they just fix the broken bones? Why did they have to cut his arm off?" asked Tom.

"Oh, they fixed his arm, all right," said Melissa. "But, on the way home from the hospital, that same damn horse ran in front of his car. He was only using one arm to drive and he was driving way too fast. So, when he swerved to miss the horse, he drove into a deep ditch."

"Why wasn't Grandma driving?" asked Big John.

"Your Grandma didn't drive and you know how stubborn he was. He didn't even tell her what had happened. When that horse trampled on his arm, he just got up, walked down the hill to his car, got in, and drove to the hospital. Sometimes I forget what a tough old bird he was," answered Melissa.

"Well, if he just drove into a ditch, why did he lose his arm?" asked Tom.

"The car flipped when it hit the ditch and landed driver's side down. He was on Clinton Road and he knew no one would be coming by to help him. He lay there, in that upside-down car, trying to figure out what to do. He tried blowing the horn, hoping someone would hear it and come help him. That didn't do no good, though. Your Grandma finally got worried because she couldn't find him and called a neighbor. The neighbor decided to drive over to the house and, after he drove a little way down Clinton Road, he saw your grandpa's car in the ditch," Melissa said.

"For crying out loud, Mother. How did he lose his arm?" yelled Big John.

"The neighbor couldn't get him out of the car. He was pinned in. He had the windows open when he flipped the car and his broken arm was now pinned between the ditch and the car. The weight of the car had splintered the cast and his arm was a bloody mess," Melissa continued.

"You never told me this story. I never heard this story before," exclaimed Big John.

"Well, the neighbor went to the house and told your grandma to call the ambulance and the fire department. He grabbed a bottle of Jack Daniels off the counter and went back to wait with your grandpa. After about half an hour, here they come, sirens blaring, horns honking, the whole show. It was pretty exciting."

"You were there, mom?" asked Tom.

"Oh, ya. I was about fifteen at the time. I'll never forget that night. Your grandma was worried to death and pacing the floor. She wouldn't go down to the car. She was too upset. Mary Ellen was about five and, I remember, your grandma asked me to put her to bed. I just ignored her. It was dark out by now, but I threw on a jacket and ran down the road. When I got to the car, your grandpa yelled at me to get back to the house."

"Did you? Did you go back to the house?" asked Bobby.

"Hell, no. I stayed right there and watched. I'll never forget it. They needed to jack up the car in order to get his arm free. They had lots of lights shining on the car, so they could see what they were doing. But that big old car was so far down in the dirt in that ditch they couldn't get the jack in place. After a lot of discussions, they decided to cut the metal away on both sides of the window where his arm was stuck. When the fireman who was using that saw, or whatever they call that thing they use, started to cut away part of the car, it slipped. He cut grandpa's arm right off."

"Holy shit!" said Tom.

"Holy shit is right. I'll never forget that night. You know what else I'll never forget?"

"What's that, Mom," said Big John.

"I'll never forget how absolutely gullible y'all are," Melissa said, laughing.

"You just made that up? That's not what happened?" said Bobby.

"It was a good story, though, wasn't it? I sure had you guys going for a while. Well, here we are. Clinton Road. Let's go see what's in the frig. I hope he has some beer. I could sure use a cold one right about now," said Melissa.

"Sounds good," Bobby replied.

"We should take a good look around and see if there's anything we want to take home with us before Mary Ellen gets it all," she added.

"What happened to the horse?" asked Tom.

Melissa pulled the car up to the front of the house and turned off the key. Memories started flooding back from the time she spent in this house. It was too bad they weren't good memories. She had only been back a couple of times to visit since she left twenty-seven years ago. The last time she was here was for her mother's funeral.

The boys jumped out of the car and ran up the steps to the front porch. Bobby tried to open the door but found it locked.

"It's locked, Ma. Guess we'll have to wait until Mary Ellen and Peter get here to let us in," he said.

"Well, I gotta pee and I'm not going sit around here outside with all these mosquitoes. Check under that cement planter there in front of you. Grandpa used to keep a spare key there."

"Found it," said Bobby, holding up the key to show it to his mom.

"Well, then, open the damn door."

Once inside, they made themselves at home. Melissa used the bathroom to relieve herself. After she washed her hands, she checked to see what was in the medicine cabinet. My god, she thought, there's every pain pill in here that you can think of. I wonder what was wrong with daddy that he had to take all these pills.

Melissa wandered from room to room, checking them out. Not much here I want, she thought. It looks like he hasn't bought anything new since I was last here. The problem with old furniture is that it never wears out. Mary

Ellen can have all this junk.

Melissa walked into the living room where her three sons were sprawled on the furniture, drinking beer.

"Big John, go get me one of those," she said, as she dropped into a big oversized chair.

"There isn't any more left," he said.

"Are you friggin' kidding me?"

Five

Melissa got out of the chair, walked to the kitchen, and checked the inside of the refrigerator. Tom was right. No more beer. She grabbed a can of pop, opened it, went back into the living room, and sat down.

As she looked around the room, she focused in on an old grandfather's clock standing in the corner. "I want that clock," she said, to no one in particular.

"What'd you say, Mama?" asked Big John.

"I want that clock over there. I don't want anything else in this house, just that clock. Put it in the car."

"We can't take that back to Hollister with us. There won't be room for all of us with that in the car."

"Well, then, I guess we'll have to put one of you on the roof. One way or the other, that clock is going home with me. Sounds like a car pulling up. I guess Mary Ellen and Peter are here."

A few seconds later, Mary Ellen walked in, obviously upset. "How the hell did you get in? This house was locked. What'd you do? Break a window? Would be just like you to do something like that."

"Don't get your undies in a bundle, Mary Ellen. We used a key. Daddy kept a spare key under the planter."

"Oh, that's right. Sorry for yelling. It's been a rough day."

"Where's Peter? I thought he would be with you."

"We got into a fight. He went home," Mary Ellen replied.

"Man, is there a time when you two don't fight? Never mind about that, right now. When is the Will going to be read?" asked Melissa.

"The reading of the Will takes place the day after the funeral," said Mary Ellen.

"So, when's the funeral? I hope it's tomorrow 'cause we gotta get back home. The boys have jobs they gotta get back to, you know," Melissa said.

"The funeral is going to be on Friday. We are going to wake him the night before and for a couple of hours before the funeral. I hope you all brought some nice clothes with you," said Mary Ellen.

"What the hell, Mary Ellen? We can't sit around here for the next five days. We're going to spend the night and head home in the morning. We'll come back up for the funeral, but we gotta get back home."

"I could use some help, Melissa. You and the boys could stay around and help me with the arrangements. Maybe cut the grass and clean up the yard a little."

"Sorry, we'll be gone in the morning. I'll drive back up on Thursday for the funeral. And, by the way, I'm taking the clock over there with me. You can have all the rest of this crap."

"Like hell you are. Nobody gets anything until the

lawyer reads daddy's Will. You can't just take stuff."

"Well, I didn't know that. I'm going to bed. It's been a long day and we're all tired. I'll call you in the morning before we leave. Good night, Mary Ellen."

Mary Ellen stood up, gave her sister a look that could kill, and walked out the door.

Melissa stood watching the car go down the driveway. As soon as the taillights on Mary Ellen's car were no longer visible, she turned and looked at her boys.

"Tom, you hold the door. Bobby and Big John, you two pick up that clock and put it in the car. And, be damn sure you don't' scratch it."

Six

Melissa laughed to herself every time she glanced in the rear-view mirror and saw Tom and Bobby. The boys had folded the back seat and the third seat flat to be able to get the grandfather clock in the SUV. That hadn't left much room for the two boys, who were lying side by side next to the clock.

That has to be uncomfortable, Melissa thought. She had been driving for almost four hours. It was time to pull over at the next rest stop, so they could stretch their legs. She glanced over at Big John who was sharing the front seat with her. He was sound asleep. Maybe I should stick him in the back for a while and have Bobby sit up front with me.

"Rest stop coming up, boys. We'll take a break. Wake up, Big John."

"I'm hungry. When can we stop and get something to eat?" asked Bobby.

"You're always hungry. Okay, I'll stop at the next town, so we can get something to eat. You can stretch your legs there."

Thirty minutes later, she pulled off the highway to gas up and get something to eat. The entire time they ate, Tom and Bobby complained about being stuck in the back of the car with the clock.

"Get over it," Melissa said. "A few more hours and we'll

be home."

"Mom, do you have a Living Will? You know, like instructions if something happened to you. Would you want to be kept alive by machines?" Big John asked.

"Hell, no, I don't want to be kept alive. Tell you what, Big John. If that ever happens, just take a pillow and smother me. Just make sure no one is watching."

"You're kidding, right? That's a big thing to ask."

"How about you, Tom? Would you put your old mom out of her misery?"

"No problem. I'm your guy," Tom said laughing.

"I figured you would be," muttered Melissa.

"You serious, Mom? You would want Tom to do that?" asked Bobby.

"Don't get any ideas, you three. I'm just kidding."

Three hours later, they were turning off onto Business Hwy. 65. Not far to go now, she thought. Just across the Taneycomo Bridge, then Hollister and home.

Tom's voice brought her back to reality when he asked, "How much money do you think we're going to get?"

"You actually waited until we were almost home before you brought up money. I figured that would be all you would talk about on the way home. What's your guess? How much do you think I--not we--will get?"

"I figure it has to be a few hundred thousand," said Tom.

"More than that," said Bobby. "Just the land is worth more than that."

"I figure a million," said Big John.

"Or," said Melissa, "It could be nothing."

"What do you mean nothing?" said Tom. "He had to leave you half, don't you think?"

"He never forgave me for marrying your dad and moving away. He didn't like me very much. Mary Ellen could get it all. I could be left with nothing."

"Yes, I see. Is that right? When will this take place? That soon? So, it will be distributed as the funds come in. When will you mail that out? Thank you so much."

Melissa hung up her new phone. Her knees were shaking so badly she couldn't stand. She had just talked to her father's attorney. He told her that she did not have to be present for the reading of the Will, even though it was unusual when the beneficiaries didn't show up. He said he would send her a copy of the Will along with some legal forms she needed to sign and return to him.

Although he couldn't give her an exact amount, he estimated that, after taxes, her share of the estate would be around seven and a half million dollars. He had left Mary Ellen his properties and personal belongings. Everything else he had left to her.

The lawyer told her that as he liquidated stocks, bonds,

and all the other savings and investments, he would be sending her the funds. The cash from savings and checking accounts would start arriving within a few weeks. He figured that amount to be a little over seven hundred thousand dollars.

I'm going to faint, she thought. Why in the world would he do this? Maybe the attorney got Mary Ellen and me mixed up. Poor Peter. He stayed with her for all these years, hoping to get rich someday, and now this. She won't have any money until she sells the property. She'll be stuck with the upkeep of the farm, the taxes, and all the other expenses.

She picked up the phone and dialed Mary Ellen.

"I'm not coming back up for the funeral," she said when her sister answered the phone. "It's too long a drive and I already talked to the attorney and he's sending me a copy of the Will. I don't have to be present for its reading.

"You took the fucking clock? Do you know I could have you arrested for stealing?" was all Mary Ellen said.

"Oh, get over it. You would have just sold it or thrown it out. Looks like you got the short end of the stick with daddy. Let me know if I can help you out."

"Seriously, Melissa? Do you have any idea how much daddy's properties are worth? The farm has over 1,000 acres. I already have a buyer who wants to buy it so he can build a sub-division. I think I'm going to do just fine with an acre of land going for around seventy-six hundred dollars.

That's just the farm. He has other properties. You probably didn't know that, seeing as how you weren't around that much."

"Well, I'm happy for you," said Melissa.

"You know what, Melissa, I'm glad you're not coming to the funeral. I don't care. I don't even want you and your lazy kids there anyway. Just stay where you are in that piece of crap trailer you live in. It's where you belong," said Mary Ellen.

"It's not a trailer," yelled Melissa. "It's a mobile home."

"Whatever you call it, it's still a crap trailer. Good-bye."

"Bitch!" Melissa yelled and started to throw the phone, and then thought better about it. She put the handset back onto the phone's base.

Screw her and her thousand acres, she muttered to herself.

Seven

On Wednesday afternoon, Melissa drove to the restaurant where she worked in Branson and gave her two-week notice. Then, she drove to the Walmart Supercenter and bought seven of the biggest porterhouse steaks she could find. After stopping at the liquor department for a couple of six-packs of beer, she topped her cart off with some potato salad and ice cream. Before the boys left the house that morning, she had mentioned that they should try to be home in time for dinner.

All three boys were there when she arrived home. Bobby came running out of the house to greet her and asked, "Can I help you with the groceries, Mom?"

"Sure, sweetie. The bags are in the trunk. Thank you so much."

Melissa threw him the keys and walked into the house, leaving him to carry in the bags. She smiled to herself, thinking how fast things can change when money is involved. She couldn't remember the last time one of her sons had offered to carry in the groceries, much less come running out of the house to greet her.

"Big John, I bought some nice porterhouse steaks for dinner. Perhaps you will do us the honor of grilling them in a little while?" she said

"Be happy to, Mom. Did you buy any beer?" he replied.

"Sure did. Why don't you go help Bobby unpack the groceries and then bring me one?"

"Happy to, Mom."

A few minutes later Bobby and Big John joined Tom and Melissa in the living room. Big John handed his mom a beer and sat down.

"Something you want to talk about, Mom?" he asked.

"I've got some news. Yesterday I called and talked to your Aunt Mary Ellen. I told her that we wouldn't be back up for the funeral on Friday."

"Thank goodness," said Bobby. "I was having nightmares just thinking about taking that ride back up there."

"I probably won't be hearing from her for a while. She was really upset. She even threatened to have me arrested because I took the clock."

"But, now that Grandpa's dead, doesn't his stuff belong to you? I suppose you have to split it, but you would have got the clock anyway," said Big John.

"No. According to the lawyer, Mary Ellen gets all his personal belongings. In a sense, I guess I did steal it. But she gets all the other stuff, so I'm glad I took it. At least I have one thing to cherish that belonged to my mama and him."

She watched her son's faces as the words started to sink in. My god, she thought, Tom's gonna cry. Bobby's gonna blow any minute now, and Big John looks like he just ate rotten fish.

"Now, before you get all upset and start to lose it, I have more to tell you. I talked to your grandpa's lawyer yesterday. He told me what is in Grandpa's Will."

"Mary Ellen gets it all, right?" said Bobby.

"Wrong. You know that Mary Ellen and Peter never had kids. I guess your grandpa thought it wouldn't be fair if you boys received a share. Wouldn't make it equal, you know. None of you will get anything. Mary Ellen gets all his properties and belongings and he left me all the money. She comes out a little ahead, but it's pretty even."

"Do you know how much?" asked Big John.

"It will take some time before all the figures are put together. I'll get some of it in a few weeks. The rest will dribble in as accounts are closed and stocks are sold and stuff. I'm getting a copy of the Will. Her attorney is also sending an itemized list of all the assets. It's looking pretty good."

"Do you have an estimate, Mama? Any idea?" asked Big John.

"Looks like around seven to eight million. That's after taxes. That's what I'll actually get."

It was as if someone sucked all the air out of the room. Her sons were in shock - for about fifteen seconds. Then, they were on their feet, dancing around in a circle, laughing, and yelling, "We're rich, we're rich".

Big John grabbed his mother, picked her up out of her chair, and swung her around. "All our problems are over, Mama. We can buy anything we want now. Cars, houses, boats, new clothes, anything we want."

"Put me down, Big John. Enough, boys. Sit down. You are not rich. I am rich. You have the same amount of money right now as you did a few minutes ago."

"Well, ya, Mom, but you're gonna give us some, right?" said Tom.

"I don't know. It's gonna depend on you. Some things might change, but not for a while. It's all gonna depend on you."

"I don't get it," said Bobby. "What are you talking about?"

"Here's the deal. Listen up, 'cause you're gonna be the ones deciding if you get anything. Tom, go get me another beer. This one's warm. From now on, I don't have to drink warm beer."

"You know, boys, with a lot of money, comes a lot of responsibility," she continued. "This money is my freedom to do whatever I want. When I die, it will be your freedom. If you use it wisely, it can be your children's freedom. No, sirree, we aren't going to blow it. We're gonna be smart."

"Well, of course, we aren't going to blow six million dollars, but we're going buy a new house and some cars and stuff, right?" asked Tom.

"Probably closer to seven," replied Melissa. "Boys, come outside with me."

Melissa walked to the door and waited. Her boys didn't move.

"Now!"

If a firecracker had been set off under their butts, they couldn't have moved any faster. In seconds, they were all outside.

"Come with me," said Melissa and went down the front steps and across the lawn to the road. She turned and looked at her home. "What do you see, boys? Tell me exactly what you see."

"A dump. That's what I see. An old trailer that should be torn down," said Tom.

"I see what Tom sees," said Bobby. "An old worn-out piece of crap that's on its last legs."

"Tom, that's the second time in two days that you called your home a dump," said Melissa. "What about you, Big John? What do you see?"

"I see a trailer......."

"It's a mobile home. Not a trailer," yelled Melissa.

"Sorry, Mom. I see a mobile home that has seen a lot of neglect. It's dirty, needs a lot of repairs, and has probably outlived its usefulness," said Big John.

"You know what I see?" asked Melissa. "Memories. This is where your daddy and I started our married life. It's where all you boys were born, took your first steps, and said your first words. After your daddy left, it became a happy home. I still like to think that it's a happy home. Your right, Big John, I have neglected it. Raising you three boys hasn't been easy. I could hardly afford to feed you much less have money for anything extra. Now I do."

"You did a good job, mom. You did the best you could," said Bobby.

"Why, thank you, son. I appreciate that. Now, here's what I plan on doing. First of all, you don't have to move out in a couple of weeks. I know the three months are almost up, but things have changed. Don't get me wrong. You can still leave if you want to."

"I want to stay, Mama. I didn't want to leave anyway. You know that," said Tom.

Ignoring him, Melissa continued. "I'm not moving. Perhaps, I will down the road, but I'm staying right here for now. You boys are going to fix up this place. The roof is going to be replaced, you are going to power wash the outside, the skirting needs to be replaced, and so do the shutters. That poor excuse that passes for front steps needs to be replaced. You can build those in no time."

"But, Mom, you can hire someone to do all that. Why should we do it?" asked Tom.

Ignoring him once more, Melissa said, "Then, there's the yard. We are going to have a beautiful lawn with some flowerbeds. A few of the trees need to be trimmed back and I figure you boys should be able to do that."

"I don't get it," said Bobby. "This stuff wasn't' taken care of because you couldn't afford to hire someone to do it. Now that you can afford it, you want us to do it. That's crazy."

"Here's the deal. You have six months to…….."

"Six months?" interrupted Tom. "You expect us to do all this in six months."

"Do not interrupt me again. Let me finish," snapped Melissa.

"Here's the deal. You have six months to get all this done. I'm giving each one of you $3,500.00. With this money, you will pay for all the repairs. If you have anything left over, you can keep it."

"Do we still have to keep our jobs?" asked Bobby.

"You better, because I'm not supporting you," Melissa answered.

"This will take all of our spare time," whined Tom.

"Tom, quit your belly aching and let me finish. You guys can decide what you want to do," said Melissa. "If you can show me that you can do this, I will give each one of you enough for a down payment on a house. Tom, you're going to be a daddy by then and ….."

"No, I'm not. Molly and I broke up."

"Not the daddy?"

"She was never pregnant. Just using me," said Tom.

"Probably for the best. Anyway, as I was saying, I will give each one of you enough money for a down payment, so you can buy your own place. Twenty thousand dollars each."

"What if we don't want to buy a house? I don't know if I can afford a mortgage. I don't even have a job. What then? Will you still give us the money? Can I still stay here and live with you?" asked Tom.

"No, I won't and no, you can't. In six months, either you move into a house that you buy with the twenty thousand I give you or you find a place to live and move out. Either way, you're gone. Property, boys. The best investment you can make is in real estate. Daddy just taught me that."

"You just inherited over seven million dollars and we only get twenty thousand? That's wack," said Tom.

"Take it or leave it, boys. You'll get what's left when I die, but not today. I'm going back inside. You think about it."

The three boys didn't speak as Melissa went up the old broken-down steps and back into the house. Bobby swore silently under his breath. Tom just shook his head in disbelief. Big John looked at his two brothers and said," I swear, someday I'm gonna kill that woman."

Eight

Melissa's sons had gone to Waxy's, a bar near Branson Landing, to have a beer. They needed to get away from Melissa and go where they could talk in private.

No one said anything until after the waitress had taken their order. "What are we going to do?" asked Tom. "I never figured this would happen. I don't want to buy a house. I mean, I want a house, but I don't think I should have to pay for it. Mom could just buy it outright and give it to me. What's she gonna do with all that money, anyway? I can't figure out what's going on in that head of hers."

"It's a test," said Bobby. "I think she's testing us to see if we take her offer or walk away. If we don't do it, then she won't even give us the thirty-five hundred."

"Big deal. We're supposed to use that money to fix the trailer. It will probably cost more than that just to fix the roof," Tom replied.

"We can do all that shit in six months, no problem. We show her that we want to help and I'll bet you the toes off a goat that she'll give us some money. What do you think, Big John?" Bobby asked.

"She's talking about $10,500.00 to fix everything. I'm pretty sure we can do that and still have some left over. But, that's not the point. I know that woman and she has something else up her sleeve. I can smell it."

"Perhaps, we should just all move out and get our own places," said Bobby. "Hell, Big John, you're going on thirty and still living with mama. Maybe, she's just tired of us and this is her way of getting us out."

"When mama gets fixated on something, she doesn't let go. That comment about real estate. I have this weird feeling that she's gonna start spending that money on land."

"Well, she could buy Branson with all that money," said Tom.

"No, Tom, she couldn't. But, she sure as hell could buy a lot of it," Big John replied.

"She's got something in mind. She's still a young woman. How much you wanna bet, when word gets around that she's rich now, she'll have a boyfriend in no time?" asked Tom.

"I guess any guy will overlook those scars if he thinks he can land mama and all her money. That cut on her cheek went deep. What happened anyway? She won't say anything. Bobby, you know what happened?" said Big John.

"All she said was she cut herself. She sure is accident-prone. At this rate, she'll kill herself," commented Bobby.

"And, save us the trouble," said Tom.

"It's gonna be a few weeks or more before she starts seeing any of that money. I think we should all go along with her plan and see how it plays out," said Big John. "We know she changes her mind all the time. Let's not forget that mama isn't stupid. In the meanwhile, we can show her we're taking her serious. Making plans on how to fix things, where to buy the materials, and that kinda shit. But she worries me, boys. I'm afraid that we might not see any of that money until she's gone and we're old men."

"What about what you said at the house?" asked Tom.

"What - about killing her?"

"Ya, what about that?" answered Tom.

"Said in anger, Tom. I didn't mean it. Right now, we need to keep all of our options open and our mouths shut. The fewer people who know about mama's newfound wealth, the better."

"Ready for another beer?" asked Bobby. "My treat."

"Sure am," answered Tom. "Always ready for another one."

While her sons were discussing their future, Melissa was on her computer checking out financial advisors. Her mind was going a mile a minute, thinking about all the things she needed to do. Tomorrow she would drive to her bank and get information about the different types of accounts they offered. Then, she needed to find out what land was for sale around the area.

Best she could tell, farming plus buying property was how her father had made his money. She planned to double her wealth soon. Buy low and sell high. She had heard that somewhere but wasn't sure if it referred to land. Damn, she was gonna be rich. Just the thought of it almost brought tears to her eyes.

I've been poor almost my entire life, she thought. I raised those boys with little or no help. Now, it's my time. I have enough money so I never have to work again. I guess I could give more to the boys right away, but they need to know what it's like to struggle. If I had told them I was giving each of them a million dollars, they still wouldn't be happy. As long as I have it, they're going to want it all.

I need to make a Will. Better put that on the list of things to do, she thought.

Melissa glanced down at the pad of paper on the table and picked up her pen. Man, she thought, this list is getting longer and longer.

A noise woke her at 12:15 a.m. She sat up in bed and listened. It was those damn boys. She got out of bed, opened her bedroom window, and yelled, "Will you all shut your sorry asses up and get in here. I'm trying to sleep and you have to go to work in the morning. Well, at least two of you do."

"Coming, Mother," said Bobby, which cracked up his brothers.

"For crying out loud, get in here," Melissa said, as she slammed the window shut. "Stupid idiots," she muttered to herself.

She heard the front door open and close. Being satisfied that the foolishness was probably over for the night, she rolled over and went back to sleep.

As Bobby walked through the kitchen on the way to his room, he noticed a pad of paper on the kitchen table. As he glanced down at it, he read the heading on the first sheet of paper. She had written 'Things To Do ASAP' and had underlined it three times.

"Big John, Tom, look at this," he said to his brothers. "Mom made a list and right here it says to make a Will."

"Let me see," said Big John. He picked up the pad of paper and started reading it. "Look here," he said. "She scratched it off the bottom of the list and put it at the top."

"Maybe she just put it down twice and then scratched one off," said Tom.

"Whatever," said Bobby, "It's at the top of her list. I wonder what she is planning to do with that money."

"I don't know why we're all worried about this. Who else is she gonna give it to if not us?" said Tom.

"I don't know," replied Big John. "I got me a real bad feeling about this. We gotta be smart, boys. We just gotta stay smart."

Nine

When Melissa got up the next morning, she was surprised to see Tom out of bed and sitting at the kitchen table. She noticed that her pad of paper was still where she had left it the night before. Well, that's suspicious, she thought. No way the boys didn't see it laying there. Looks like they were pretty careful to put it back exactly where it was.

"Whatcha doing, Tom?" she said to her son. "You look pretty absorbed in something."

Tom jumped a little, pretending he was startled by the sound of her voice. "Morning, Mama," he said. "You scared me. I'm just making a list of all the things we're going to need to start all those projects. We talked about it last night and we think it's a good idea to fix the place up. I'm just making a list of supplies. We're going to start with the easy stuff and finish with the roof. Of course, the yard will be a challenge and we might need some people to help with that. We'll need some good brown dirt for the flowerbeds and we were thinking that it might be nice to lay sod. Our grass is bad and sod would look nice. We would have to get a lot of dirt if we do that. Would you like that or just do the flower beds?"

"My goodness. You boys were busy last night. I haven't thought about sod. That's an excellent idea. Tell you what,

Tom. You find out how much extra that is and I'll add it to the money I give you boys.

"Well, we also have another idea. We all just kinda park our trucks anywhere. We thought that we could take that area over on the east side of the trail..., excuse me, mobile home and smooth it out and bring in a couple loads of gravel and make it our parking area. We want to put a fence around the yard. That way no one will park on the grass anymore."

"My, my, my. So ambitious you all are. But I won't need that parking area if you boys are all going to move to your own houses. A fence would be nice though."

"What if we all visit you at the same time? Or, you have company? It would be a real nice place to park, don't ya think?"

"You boys think you can get all this done in six months? That seems like a lot of work when you only have weekends. Well, your brothers only have weekends and I guess they can do some of it after they get home from work. You could spend your days doing this stuff instead of bumming around."

"Anyway, Mom, I'm trying to figure out the cost to do all this. I just don't think what you are planning to give us is going to cut it. I think we can do it all for around twenty. Why don't we just get the stuff done and you pay for the supplies?" Tom asked. "Let's just forget about that thirty-five hundred each deal."

"That deal," Melissa replied, "Was to make you show me that you could work within a budget. What's it going to accomplish if I just pay for everything?"

"Why don't we just make the budget twenty thousand and make sure we do all this for that amount? If we come in under, then we get to keep whatever is left over," Tom said. "And, the six months starts when we get some money to work with."

"The reading of the Will is tomorrow. The lawyer told me that as soon as that is over, he could start liquidating and send me some funds. I could speed up the process by setting up an account at Lowes, so you can start buying supplies now."

"So, you're going to agree to the twenty?" asked Tom.

"Seems fair with all the work you're gonna do. Ya, I'll agree to that. I'll drive over to Lowes and set that up later today. Looks like you made a pot of coffee. Sure, smells good."

"That's the least I could do after waking you up last night. Sorry about that, Mom."

Later that day, Melissa drove to the bank and opened an interest-bearing savings account. The interest that would be earned was negligible, but Melissa didn't plan to keep the money there for any length of time. She talked to the manager and asked if he could give her the name of a financial advisor. He told her that they had someone that worked with the bank and he would have him give her a call to set up an appointment.

She drove to Lowes and applied for credit. The manager told her she would have to open a credit card account. She filled out the paperwork and found out that her limit was only five thousand dollars. That would have to do for now. The boys would have to limit their spending to that amount until she had some cash in the bank.

Her last stop before going home was at Liberty Star Realty. She knew Jimmy McKnight, from working at the restaurant, and wanted to talk to him. He wasn't in so she left a message asking him to call her.

Tom was coming out of the shed when she drove up to the house. He waved hello and waited until she parked her car.

"Just checking to see what tools we have. It looks like we're going to have to pick up a few essentials to do all this work," he told his mom, as she got out of the car.

"I set up an account at Lowes. I won't get the actual card for a few days, but you can use the account number to pick up a few things. Just start with the small jobs that won't cost much. My limit is only five thousand dollars, so that's all you can put on the card. After that, we have to wait until I get some money from the attorney. Then, we'll pay for everything in cash."

"Great. I'm on my way," said Tom.

"Where you going?" Melissa asked.

"I'm starting now. I'm on my way to Lowes."

"Really. You know what you need?"

"My first project is simple and it's not going to cost a lot."

With that, Tom ran into the house, grabbed his car keys, jumped in his pickup, and went tearing down the road.

I don't believe I've ever seen that boy move so fast, thought Melissa. I wonder how he plans to buy anything without the account information. I swear, if that boy had a lick of brains, he'd be dangerous.

A couple of hours later, Melissa watched as Tom unloaded his truck. As far as she could tell, all he had bought was just a bunch of boards. Wonder what he plans on doing with those, she thought to herself. Whatever. I'm staying out of it. This is their project and the minute I say anything, there'll be a battle.

Ten

The next morning, Melissa felt anxious. Today was the day the Will was being read, and she was having second thoughts about not going back up to Illinois to attend the meeting. I'm being silly, she thought. The lawyer already told me everything that was in it. All I have to do now is just sit back and wait for the money to roll in.

She did a little light cleaning, threw a load of dirty clothes in the washer, and decided to run to Walmart to pick up some groceries. She grabbed her purse, headed out the door - and fell five feet onto the cement slab where the stairs used to be.

She yelled for Tom, who was in the shed. She tried to sit up, but her back was hurting and she could feel the blood running down her face.

"Mom, what happened?" he yelled as he rounded the corner of the house.

"If I could stand right now, I'd kick your ass all the way down the road and drown you in Lake Taneycomo. What does it look like happened? There are no fucking stairs. Where the hell are the stairs?"

"You're bleeding pretty bad, Mom. I think I should take you to the emergency room."

"I hit my face when I landed. I think I broke my nose."

"You have to get it looked at. Get in the truck."

"Do you suppose you could help me up? Go get some towels."

"What do you want me to do first? Help you up or get the towels?" asked Tom

"Maybe you should help me get in the truck first and then get the towels. Otherwise, you'll just drive off with them and forget about me."

Four hours later Melissa was back at home. Her nostrils were packed with gauze and she had tape across the bridge of her nose to hold it in place. Both her eyes were already starting to turn purple. The doctor had told her to take acetaminophen for the pain, ice, stay home, rest, and no heavy lifting. He also told her that, when the swelling went down, he would determine if surgery would be needed to straighten her nose.

Bobby and Big John were not kind to her when she walked in the door.

"Whatcha do, Mom? Stick your face in the garbage disposal?" said Bobby as he laughed.

"My God, you look like something out of a horror movie," chimed in Big John. "You're gross. Better stay away from little kids or they'll have nightmares."

"Aren't you a couple of comedians? Help me sit down, Tom. My back is killing me. Everyone, sit," she said. "Bobby, sit your butt down. I have something to say."

"Did you hear from the attorney? Did he send any money yet?" asked Bobby.

"I see the doctor took your stitches out. That's gonna leave a real nice scar," said Big John.

"Will you just shut up and listen," Melissa said. "Yes, the doctor took my stitches out. He figured as long as I was in the emergency room, he would save me a trip, so he removed them.

"Did it hurt much?" asked Bobby.

"Bobby, look at me. My entire face hurts. I've got scrapes and bruises all over my body. My nose is broke. I've wrenched my back. Do you really think that having a few stitches removed was a big deal?"

"Now," she continued, "I would appreciate it if you boys would inform me of any future projects that are in progress. Starting tomorrow, I want a note on the refrigerator telling me what projects you are working on. If you finish one job, scratch it off the list. If you start a new job, add it to the list. I want to know what you are doing, so I know where it is safe for me to walk. Tom, no more surprises. If I didn't know better, I'd swear you are trying to kill me. Understood?"

No one spoke.

"Do you understand?" she yelled. "Answer me."

"Yes, mama," they replied in unison.

With that said, Melissa slowly rose off the chair. "I'm going to bed," she said. "No noise from any of you.

Understood?"

"Yes, mam," said Big John.

"Yes, mama,' replied Bobby.

"Okay, dokay," said Tom, with a big smile. "Love ya, Mom."

Melissa stood there, looking at her three sons. They're still little boys, she thought. They look like grown men. They're all tall and handsome, but they act like ten-year-old kids. Perhaps boys never grow up. I sure as all shooting don't know if mine will.

"Mama, what's wrong," asked Bobby, bringing her back to reality.

"Nothing, sweetie. I was just remembering when you all were little boys. Seems just like yesterday."

Once Melissa was in her room and had closed the door, Big John looked at Tom and asked, "What the hell happened? You took away the steps and didn't tell her? What if she had landed headfirst? My god, Tom, she could have been killed."

"And, then we'd all be rich. We talked about this. You both agreed we needed to do something," Tom argued.

"You idiot. We talked about going along with her plan. We did not agree to kill her," replied Big John.

"I'm not waiting until I'm sixty years old to get that money. One way or the other, she's dead," said Tom.

"You need to back off, Tom," threatened Big John.

"Or, what?" asked Tom.

"Just back off."

*

Eleven

Melissa didn't leave her bed the next day, except to go to the bathroom. She never thought an entire body could hurt so much all at once. She ached from the top of her head to the bottom of her feet.

It was Saturday and the boys had spent most of the day outside working. Occasionally, one of them would stop in and ask her if she needed anything. The hydrocodone she had taken was working so well that even the pounding of the hammers, right outside her bedroom window, didn't keep her awake. She slept most of the day away.

Around five, Bobby came into her room with a sandwich and a glass of root beer. "You shouldn't take that pain killer on an empty stomach, Ma," he said. "Eat something. You'll feel better."

"I don't think I'm ever gonna feel better," Melissa replied. "I feel like I've been run over by a truck."

"Just eat something and go back to sleep."

"Thanks."

"We're gonna go get something to eat. We won't be gone long. We finished the front stairs. I think you're gonna like what we did. We made a little porch when you come out. Like a landing. It's about eight by eight feet. All we need to do now is stain everything and that project will be done."

"That's nice," said Melissa. "You boys sure can

accomplish stuff when you put your minds to it. Drive safe."
Melissa's eyes slowly closed and she was gone.

The boys piled into Tom's truck and headed down the hilly road to the Sonic Drive-in, in Hollister.

"Mom's sleeping a lot," said Bobby. "You think she has a concussion?"

"It's probably just the meds. She didn't hit her head, just her face," said Tom.

"Well, isn't her face part of her head?" Bobby asked. "Do you have to land on the back of your head to get a concussion? Can't you get one from getting hit on any place on the head?"

"I did hear that sleeping a lot is a sign of a concussion," said Tom.

"Do you think we should go back and wake her up?" said Bobby.

"I don't think she has a concussion," said Tom.

"How do you know? You a doctor?" replied Bobby. "I think we should check on her as soon as we get home. I'm pretty sure she has a concussion."

"She hasn't got a fucking concussion. Max Birsey had a concussion and he threw up a lot. Plus, he had double vision and a lot of other shit. Mom hasn't got that," argued Tom.

"So, you think you have to have all that other stuff to have a concussion? Everybody is different, you know. Just because that stupid Max Birsey had double vision doesn't mean mom has to. Besides, he got his from jumping off a cliff into Lake Taneycomo and missing the water. He's lucky to even be alive," said Bobby.

"If you two don't shut the fuck up you are both going to wind up with a concussion. Do you understand?" Big John said in a quiet voice.

"We're just talking. What are you getting so upset about?" said Tom.

"You're idiots. You don't know what you're talking about, so just shut up. You two drive me nuts w...."

"Now you sound like mom," said Tom.

"Can you die from a concussion?" asked Bobby.

"Ya, Big John. Can you?" said Tom.

"Keep this shit up and you're going find out. Besides, Tom, isn't that what you want? So, why worry about it?" he replied.

The ringing phone brought Melissa out of her sleep into consciousness. She put the handset to her ear and said, "This better be good."

"Melissa? Is that you?" said a strange voice.

"Who wants to know?" she replied.

"It's me, Jimmy. Jimmy McKnight. You left a message for me to call you."

"I'm sorry, Jimmy. I'm not quite awake. I had a little accident yesterday and I'm still a little out of it."

"Nothing serious, I hope. So, what can I do for you?"

"I just wanted to talk to you about looking at some real estate. Maybe, some land that could be developed, later on down the road. Or, perhaps a business that might be for sale."

"Well, I don't know Melissa. You're talking about some pretty big numbers here."

"You let me worry about that. I just want you to start looking around and let me know what's available in the area."

"I could meet with you on Monday," said Jimmy. "You want to come to me or should I drive out to your place?"

"Neither. I'm going to need some healing time before I do anything," answered Melissa. "I'll give you a call when I'm feeling better."

"What about a new house? Are you looking to move? I have a lot of really nice listings if you're interested in getting out of that trailer."

"It's a mobile home, Jimmy. And, no, not right now. Right now, my house is suiting me just fine. I'll call you in a week or so. Thanks for calling."

"Bye, Melissa. You take care of yourself, now. Hear?"

"Bye,   now."

Twelve

"We can't buy anything else for now," said Bobby. "We don't have any credit left on the Lowe's card."

Two weeks had passed since Melissa's fall. The black and blue bruises were starting to disappear and most of them had turned a yellow-green color. The doctor had told her that her nose was straight and she wouldn't need surgery. Except for some minor back pain, she was feeling pretty good.

Tom had spent every day working on the house, while his brothers were at work. Now, all three of them were standing around in the kitchen, having a beer. Melissa, who was sitting at the kitchen table, glanced over at the list on the refrigerator.

"Big John, hand me that list," she said.

He walked over to the refrigerator, grabbed the paper, and handed it to her.

"You've scratched off a lot already. Things are moving along. At this rate, you'll be done in no time at all. I gotta hand it to you. You boys are doing good."

"We've finished the front steps except for staining. We have to leave that until the end. The old shutters and skirting are gone. We'll put the new ones on after the house is power washed. We got blue shutters, Mama. That should go nice with our white trailer and it will be a nice change," said Bobby.

"I talked to Pete at the shop and he recommended a guy who does roofing. He thinks it would be best to use asphalt shingles," said Big John. "That's going to be the biggest expense. It's going run around five thousand dollars."

"Asphalt is the most expensive way to go," said Melissa.

"But, the best way to go," replied Big John. "We already rented the power washer and we are going to wash the trailer this afternoon.

Melissa sighed. "Please don't call it a trailer."

"Sorry, Mama. Then, after the new skirting and shutters are on and the roof is finished, we plan to wash it again. Should look pretty good when we are done."

"So, you need money now?" asked Melissa.

"We'll need to pay for the roof. After that, we'll have to pay for the dirt and sod and start on that.

"How about you hold off on the power washing and do it tomorrow?" she said.

"It's supposed to rain tomorrow. We'll get wet," said Tom.

"So, you're going to be outside with a hose, spraying water all over the place and you're afraid the rain will get you wet?" laughed Melissa.

"You know what?" she continued. "I haven't done anything in over two weeks. I think we should buy a couple of six-packs and go fishing. Anyone up for it?" she said.

"Hell, yes," said Bobby. "The power washing can wait until tomorrow. Great idea, Mom."

Big John owned a nice sixteen-foot Lund fishing boat that he stored at Lake Storage in Hollister. They stopped at a liquor store and bought a couple of six-packs, and then drove to get the boat. After they hitched the boat to the truck, they drove to the marina.

Now they were sitting in the middle of Lake Taneycomo, fishing poles resting comfortably on their laps. The boys were unusually quiet. Wonder what's going on in those heads, Melissa thought. Well, this is as good a time as ever to break the news. I just hope they don't capsize the boat.

"I had a bunch of money wired to me this week," she said.

Nothing. No comments.

"Did you hear what I said?" she asked.

"Ya, I heard you," answered Bobby.

"Well, don't you have anything to say?" she asked.

"We're happy for you, but it doesn't have anything to do with us. Doesn't make us any better off just 'cause you got a shitload full of money," said Tom.

"How much?" asked Big John.

"First wire transfer was over seven hundred thousand," she said. "And, that's just a start, boys. Six months from now, I'll have seven or eight million. Y'all just better hope that I don't spend it all before I die. Wouldn't it be a shame if you all wound up with nothing but the shirts on your back?"

"You know what, Mom? I've been working at Pete's since I got out of school. I'll be living on my own pretty soon. Cynthia and I are talking about getting married and the two of us are going to be just fine without your money."

"So, you don't want the twenty thousand for a down payment on a house, then?" asked Melissa.

"If you want to give it to me, fine. If not, that's fine, too. Just don't keep throwing it in our faces that you got money and we don't. I'm tired of hearing about it."

"You can give me his share," said Tom. "I could sure use that money if he doesn't want it."

Suddenly, Bobby grabbed his pole and yelled, "I got a big one." He stood up and started reeling in the fish. The boat started to rock, as Tom stood up to get closer to Bobby.

"For god's sake, sit down," yelled Melissa. "You're going to tip the boat."

"This boat won't sink," said Big John. "Here, let me show you." He stood and now most of the weight was on the same side of the boat. "Rock it, boys. Show Mom that there's absolutely nothing to be afraid of."

"Sit your asses down," yelled Melissa.

Now the boat was rocking so hard that, with each back-

and-forth motion, water started sloshing over the sides. Just when it seemed it was going to tip over, Bobby said, "Stop, there's a boat coming."

As Big John sat back down, he said, "See, I told you it wouldn't tip. You still got that fish on your line, Bobby?"

"Lost it."

"Forget that damn fish. And, no more beer," said Melissa. "You start that engine and take me back to shore. I swear I don't know what's gotten into you three scaring me like that. You know I can't swim."

"Couldn't have another one if we wanted to," said Bobby. "We drank it all."

The house was finished. It had a new roof, a new porch and steps, new shutters, and skirting. It looked white again. Melissa stood in the yard and smiled. It looks so nice I don't know if I will ever leave here, she thought.

"So, Tom, you wanna walk me through the plans for the yard? Where are you planning on putting the flower beds?"

Melissa followed Tom around the yard as he pointed out what they planned on doing. "We thought a nice picket fence, painted blue to match the shutters. What do you think?"

Melissa thought for a minute before answering. "I like it. You have good design taste, Tom. Maybe you should do landscaping. Have you thought about trying to get a job with a landscaper?"

"You want me to cut grass and dig weeds? I don't think so," he replied.

"Just an idea. Don't get all uppity," she said.

"If you want to spend a little extra, we could put in a cement sidewalk," said Tom.

"Oh, a sidewalk. Let me think about that for a while. In the meantime, go ahead and order the dirt. We can do the parking area after everything else is finished. Okay?"

"Sounds good to me, Mom,' he replied.

Thirteen

Bobby was having a sandwich and a beer with Max Carson. The two had met for lunch and were deep in conversation.

"Bobby, you know I didn't finish law school. I'm not sure I have all the answers for you."

"I just want to know a few things about estate stuff. Just between us, my mom has come into a lot of money. My brothers and I are her only living relatives, except for her sister back in Illinois. If mama dies before making a Will, what happens to the money and stuff?"

"Well, if I remember the little law I learned, it would go into probate and then the courts decide how it would be distributed. Probate without a Will is costly. Her sister wouldn't enter into the picture at all," answered Max. "Of course, if your mom has a Will, it would make the process faster and easier. Probate without a Will can hang things up for a long time."

"How long?" Bobby asked.

"Depending on the courts, it could take months, even years."

"So, it would be better if mama has a Will?" asked Bobby.

"I think so if you figure you and your brothers are going to get everything. However, if you're worried she may leave everything to some dumb charity, like Bucky Beaver Rescue Center or Stairs Without Railings, you might hope she doesn't make one and wait for the probate court to handle it. Sometimes, it moves along quickly and sometimes it doesn't. Just no way of knowing," Max said.

"Just a toss of the coin, I guess," said Bobby.

"Just how much you talking about anyway?" asked Max.

"Between seven five and eight," said Bobby.

"Seventy-five thousand?" inquired Max.

"Million."

"Holy crap, Bobby. Are you shitting me? You damn well better hope she has a Will," exclaimed Max.

A few miles away, Melissa was going over real estate listings with Jimmy McKnight. She was sitting next to him at his desk, while he showed her listings for undeveloped land and businesses for sale.

"How much are you thinking of spending, Melissa?" he asked. "If you could give me some idea of what we're talking about, I could narrow down my search."

"I won't know until I see it," she answered. "Let's start at two to three million. That should give me an idea of what's available in that price range."

"There's a lot of undeveloped land for sale. Here's a listing right here in Hollister for twenty acres. Only one point two million. Here's a nice area overlooking Table Rock

Lake. Seventeen acres, lake front, right off Hwy. 265 for one point four."

"What about businesses?" asked Melissa.

"Pick one. There are restaurants, stores, condos, apartment buildings, hotels, and motels for sale. Want to own a Super 8? We got one for sale. Want a small hotel? Here's one for eight hundred ninety-five thousand. You know what, Melissa? I think you should go home and start looking at these on your computer. Start making notes and narrow it down to maybe ten. We could pick a day next week to take a look at some of the ones you are interested in."

"That's probably a good idea. I'm just wasting your time and mine looking at stuff that I don't even know if I'm interested in," she said. "I'll call you."

"Absolutely. I'm yours any time. Just let me know. By the way, sorry to hear about your dad," Max said.

"Thanks. I miss him so much. At least he went fast and didn't suffer much."

Tom watched his mother pull up and park in front of the trailer. Wonder what she's been up to now, he thought. The next few months should be real interesting. As her bank account grows, so will her craziness.

"Hi, Mom. Whatcha been up to?" he asked.

"Tom, I've got an idea. I've just come from the realtors and, as I was driving home, I got this great idea."

"And, just what would that be?" he asked with a dumb grin on his face. "Gonna bulldoze all the trees off the back lot and build a swimming pool?"

"A swimming pool? I never even gave that a thought. Why in the world would I want to build a swimming pool? I can't even swim."

"Maybe, if we had a pool, you would learn how," said Tom.

"That's not it. Come in the house with me. I've got an idea for you."

Melissa went inside and dropped into a chair in the kitchen. "You wanna get me a beer?" she asked Tom.

"Mom, you're sitting right next to the frig. Why can't you get it yourself?"

"Just forget it. I'm hot and tired. I'm gonna go sit in the tub for a while," she answered. "Don't want any damn beer, anyway."

"Just wait. I'll get you one. You don't have to get all huffy on me."

He opened the refrigerator door, took out a beer, and handed it to her.

"The cap, please."

"Are you fucking kidding me? Is your arm broke? Give it to me."

He grabbed the beer out of his mother's hand and turned the cap. "Here," he said and handed the bottle back to her.

"You just better watch your language, young man. You got a real smart mouth on you," said Melissa.

Tom pulled out a chair and sat down. "So, what do you wanna talk about?"

Melissa took a big slug of beer and swallowed. "God, that's good," she said. "Tom, you haven't worked in almost two years."

"I didn't know that," he said sarcastically.

"Watch it, boy," said Melissa.

"Sorry."

"I know you've tried to find a job. You would think there would be millions of jobs in Branson, but times are tough. How would you like to go back to school?"

Tom stared at her. "Would I like to do what?"

"I'm thinking you should take some business courses at a college."

"College of the Ozarks? I'd never get in there," Tom laughed. "I had horrible grades in high school. I'd never make it"

"Not there. Take some online courses and get educated in business. Take some bookkeeping classes and maybe a class or two on how to run a business."

"Seriously, mom? Just what business did you have in mind for me to run?"

"I'm going to start investing. I'm not sure yet what I'll

put some of this money into, but I just found out that there are a couple of motels for sale. The Motel 8 is for sale. If I bought it and you had some experience, I could make you the manger. You could run it for me. I'd pay you a good wage and you could buy your own place."

"How much would you pay me?" Tom asked.

"Don't put the cart before the horse. We're a long way from even discussing that," Melissa said.

"How much do the online classes cost?" he asked.

"Well, we would have to check it out. But if you promised to finish the classes - and pass them - I'll pay for them."

"Can I think about it?" Tom asked.

"I guess. Just remember that this will give you a job with enough money to buy your own place. Either way, your time living here is just about up."

Fourteen

Everyone stayed busy the following week. Big John and Bobby worked during the day at their jobs and, once they got home, spent a few hours each night working in the yard. The dirt, that needed to be put down before the sod could be laid, was about to be delivered. Tom spent most of his time digging up old grass and weeds. As soon as Big John and Bobby came home from their regular jobs, Tom would call it quits and head for the shower.

Melissa continued checking listings on the computer, trying to decide where she could invest her newfound wealth. She had spent a day with Jimmy McKnight and he showed her several vacant properties for sale. The seventeen acres of waterfront property on Table Rock Lake was a great piece of property. She started to compare every other piece of property to it and, one by one, she ruled all the others out. She definitely was leaning toward that one and she was confident she could get it for a good price. They were asking one point two million, and she figured she could get it for around nine hundred thousand.

She was disappointed when she looked at the Super 8 Motel. It was in good shape, but outdated. She would have to consider what the cost to update it would be before she made an offer – if she made an offer.

It was Friday night. The three boys had finished working

outside and were sitting at the kitchen table with Melissa.

"I understand you offered to pay for Tom to take some online classes," said Bobby.

"So," Melissa snapped.

"Nothing. I think that's really nice of you. I've been thinking of taking a few classes myself."

"What classes do you think you need?" Melissa said. "You already have a job."

"Well, maybe I don't want to sell lumber all my life. Maybe I'd like an office job. I've been thinking of doing real estate. There's good money in that. I could keep my job and take real estate classes nights and weekends," he answered.

"You know, if you become a realtor, you better have enough money to live on for at least a year. It can take that long before you might have your first closing and make some commission," said Melissa.

"How do you know so much about it?" asked Big John.

"I've been spending time with Jimmy McKnight. He told me," she answered. "What about you, Big John? Are you thinking of changing professions, too? Maybe become president of a bank or something?"

"I'm just fine, mama. I'm happy working for Pete in the shop and I'm not planning on changing a thing."

"Are you buying Tom a motel?" asked Bobby. "He said you were going buy him a motel after he finishes his classes. What do Big John and I get?"

"Well, for starters, you get to live here for the next few months, eat my food and drink my beer - all for free. That's what you get," she answered. "That's enough of this nonsense. Nobody's getting anything right now. I'm still waiting for the rest of the funds to be wired into my accounts. Well, that's not exactly true. Y'all are getting something. I got each of us a brand-new iPhone. I took out a family plan and it's unlimited minutes, so use it to your hearts' content. The best thing is that I'm paying for the service for the next five years. How, about that? You get free phones and service for five years. That should save you some money,"

"Wow! You get seven million dollars and we get a new phone", said Tom.

"You're welcome, you ungrateful little shit," Melissa said. "You don't want it, throw it in the garbage."

"Thanks, Mom," said Big John. "I appreciate it."

"Ya, Mom, that was nice of you," said Bobby.

"Well, at least two of you appreciate me," she said and walked out of the room, went into her bedroom, and shut the door behind her.

"We gotta talk," said Tom to his two brothers. "We gotta come up with a plan. I'm getting worried. Do you know if mom made a Will yet?"

"I haven't heard anything," said Bobby.

"She hasn't talked much about the money since the last

time we bitched to her about throwing it in our faces," said Big John.

"Who's her attorney?" asked Bobby.

"No idea," answered Big John.

"Where's her list of things to do? Maybe it's on there," said Tom.

"It's nowhere around here. What difference does it make?" asked Big John.

"Before we do anything drastic, we need to know if she's made a Will. I talked to Max Carson and he said that it would be in our best interests if she had a Will. Some stuff about probate. We have to find out if she's seen a lawyer," responded Bobby.

"Tom," said Bobby, "You're with her most of the day. See what you can find out."

"How we gonna do it?" asked Tom.

"Do what?" said Bobby.

"You know. You figured it out yet?"

"I'm not having this conversation. Just knock it off," Big John said softly. "What's wrong with you two, anyway?"

Fifteen

Melissa expected it to happen and it did. She knew that, as soon as word got out about her inheritance, the phone calls would start. Every Tom, Dick, and Harry, who had something to sell, tried to sell it to her. These were the easy calls. Once their pitch started in, she just slammed the phone down.

It was the calls from people she had known for almost thirty years that needed a little finesse. Women, she had little to do with, now wanted to be her best friend and Melissa was turning down one luncheon invitation after another. Men were coming out of the woodwork, calling her to ask her out for dinner or a show. Most of them she knew, some she did not. However, what she did know was that a few of them were married.

She was still in bed, looking at the ceiling and thinking it should be painted when the phone rang.

"Damn. Can't I get a minute's rest?" she muttered to herself and grabbed her phone off the nightstand.

"Do you know what the hell time it is?" she yelled into the phone.

"Melissa?" said a woman.

"Who is this?" Melissa asked.

"It's me. Mary Ellen."

"What's the matter? You sound like your crying,"

Melissa said.

"It's Peter. He left me for another woman. Can you believe that? I stick with him for all these years and now he ups and leaves me."

"Well, she must be quite the looker, if he left all that money for her."

"He's been gone for a while now. It's just that – well, the.." Sobs echoed in Melissa's ears as her sister totally lost it.

"For crying out loud, Mary Ellen. Get ahold of yourself. How long has he been gone?"

"He left about two weeks after Daddy died. He got up from the dinner table one night, told me he hated my guts, and walked out."

"So, why all the tears now?" asked Melissa.

"Because the divorce was final yesterday and the judge awarded him almost half of my money. That bastard gets almost ten million dollars," said Mary Ellen.

"How is that possi - what! Half is almost ten million dollars. Just how much money did you get from daddy?" Melissa yelled.

"That's right. You don't know. You didn't come to the reading of the Will. But I thought daddy's attorney sent you a copy."

"He did. It said you get all the properties. It didn't say what they were worth," said Melissa.

"They're worth a lot," replied Mary Ellen. "Daddy owned a whole bunch of stuff."

"So, why are you calling me?" asked Melissa.

"I was wondering if you would come and visit me. I just need to be around family and you're all I have. I'm so lonely now with daddy gone."

"Mary Ellen," said Melissa. "Right now, I am the last person you want to be around." She cut off the call and threw the phone across the room. And, ducked.

What the hell is going on now, she wondered, as she heard a loud buzzing noise coming from the front yard. She got out of bed, threw on a robe, walked into the living room, and opened the front door. And, almost peed herself.

Tom was sitting on a limb, about thirty feet up, in a big Bitternut Hickory tree. He had a chainsaw powered up and was in the process of cutting a big branch off the tree. My God, Melissa thought, he's going to kill himself. She ran under the tree and waved up at him. Tom glanced down, saw her, and turned off the saw.

"What are you doing?" she yelled up at him.

"You said you wanted some of the branches trimmed off the trees," he replied.

"Not the ones that high up. The lower branches, Tom, the lower ones."

"Oh. I thought you wanted me to thin it out all over.

Well, this branch is dead and I've cut almost all the way through it. I'll just finish it and come down. Is there any coffee?"

"Tom, you can't finish cutting it off like that."

"Why not?"

"Because you're sitting on the wrong side of the saw."

"I'm doing what?" asked Tom.

"You're going to fall with the branch."

"No. I've got it tied off. See. It's tied to the branch right below it. When the branch falls, the rope will keep it from hitting the ground. It wil......" His mother's yelling stopped him.

"You're on the wrong side! You should have your back to the trunk on the other side of the saw. You're going to come down with the branch."

Tom suddenly realized what his mother was saying. Very carefully, he started to scooch his butt over the spot where he had been cutting. He just passed the cut mark when the branch let loose, which startled him, making him drop the chainsaw.

Melissa was standing under the tree, watching Tom, when the branch broke loose. The rope attached to the branch held and it came to a stop about eight feet above the ground. Melissa, however, moved to avoid the falling branch and stepped right into the path of the falling chainsaw.

"I think we're good," yelled Tom, as he looked down at

the swinging branch. Then, he saw his mother lying face down in the dirt, the chainsaw on the ground next to her.

Tom's whole body felt weak and he wasn't sure if he could move. Finally, after taking a couple of deep breaths, he managed to stand up on what was left of the broken branch. He made his way over to the ladder and climbed down. As soon as his feet touched the ground, he was at his mother's side, taking her pulse. He couldn't find one. She's dead and I didn't even kill her, he thought.

He reached into his pocket, pulled out his cell phone, and dialed 911. After giving the emergency operator the information, he rolled his mother over onto her back.

Sixteen

Tom sat on the front steps waiting for the ambulance to arrive. His heart was pounding and his hands were shaking so badly he could hardly hold his cell phone. He punched the speed dial button and waited for Big John to answer his phone.

"What do ya want, Tom? I'm busy."

"Mom's dead, Big John. She's really dead," said Tom, and started to cry.

"What did you do?" yelled Big John.

"Nothing. I didn't do nothing. A chainsaw fell on her," Tom said.

"Say what? What fell on her?" asked Big John.

"A chainsaw. I gotta go. The ambulance is here," answered Tom, and hung up.

As the ambulance pulled into the yard, Tom ran towards it while pointing to where his mom was lying on the ground. "Over here. She's over here," he yelled as a paramedic got out of the passenger side of the vehicle.

A few seconds later, the driver exited the ambulance and walked over to Melissa, bent down to check her, and asked, "Did you move her?"

"I rolled her over, that's all. She's dead, isn't she? I couldn't find a pulse and I......" Tom broke down in tears.

"She's got a pulse. It's faint, but it's there. We're taking her to the emergency room. You want to ride with us or follow?" the paramedic asked Tom.

"Are you sure she's not dead? I thought she was dead."

"Maybe you better ride with us in the back with your mom," said the paramedic. "I don't think you should be driving."

After putting a neck brace around Melissa's neck, they carefully lifted her onto a stretcher and carried her to the ambulance. As Tom started to climb in the back, the driver stopped him. "Wait," he said to Tom, "We need to get your mother stabilized before you can get in."

Tom nodded and walked over to a tree, where he proceeded to throw up all over the ground.

Big John tried to call Tom back but didn't get an answer. He dialed Bobby's phone and it went straight to voice mail. Not knowing what else to do, he yelled at his boss that he had an emergency and would call him later.

"What happened? Where you going?" Pete asked him.

"Tom just called. Sounds like something bad happened to mom. I'm heading home."

"Go," said Pete. "Call me if you need anything."

Big John was halfway home when he saw the ambulance coming towards him, sirens blaring, lights flashing, and going way too fast. Everyone knew you had to watch your speed on these roads. Many accidents had happened when a driver misjudged his speed going around sharp curves and wound up in a ditch or headfirst into a tree.

That has to be mom in there, he thought. Big John pulled to the side, watched the ambulance go by, did a uey, and headed towards the hospital.

He arrived in time to watch his mother being wheeled through the emergency doors and into the hospital. He pulled his car into an empty spot marked 'doctors only' and jumped out. As he walked by the back of the ambulance, he saw Tom.

"What the hell is going on, Tom? Get out of there, will you?"

Tom gave his brother a blank stare. "I thought she was dead. I couldn't find a pulse," he said.

"She's not dead?" asked Big John.

"I don't think so. I don't know."

"I'm going in. You coming?" asked Big John.

Tom exited the ambulance and the two of them walked into the hospital.

Dr. Philip Wasserman saw them come in and walked over to them. "I'm beginning to think your mother should have her own room here. She seems to spend more time here than at home."

"Is she okay, doctor?" Tom said.

"The nurse is getting her cleaned up. It looks like she was hit pretty hard on the back of her neck and head with something. What happened, Big John?"

"I wasn't there. Tom was," Big John replied.

"You want to tell me what happened, Tom?" asked Dr. Wasserman.

"I was cutting a branch off a tree in our yard. The branch fell and then mom was lying on the ground."

"The branch hit her?" said Big John.

"No, the saw did. I dropped the chainsaw. When the branch broke, it scared me and I dropped the chainsaw. I guess mom moved to get out of the way of the branch and the chainsaw fell on her."

"Why was she standing under the tree?" asked the doctor.

"Because, I was facing backward and then I moved to turn around, and the branch broke off too soon, and then the chain saw dropped and...... Is she okay? I thought she was dead," replied Tom, starting to cry.

"Slow down. Was the chainsaw running when it fell?" asked the doctor.

"No, I had it turned off," replied Tom.

"Thought so. Because, if those teeth had been running when that saw hit her, they might have cut her neck clean off," said Dr. Wasserman. "Well, I have work to do. I'll see you boys later."

An hour and fifteen minutes later, Dr. Wasserman

found Big John and Tom sitting in the waiting room, both sound asleep. "Big John, wake up," he said, as he gave him a poke. "Tom, wake up."

"Tom," the doctor said, "When your mother fell, how did she land?"

"What do you mean? She landed on the ground," replied Tom.

"Face up or face down?" he asked.

"Down. She fell face-first into the dirt."

"Did you turn her over?" the doctor continued.

"Yes."

"How long before you turned her over?"

"Did I do something wrong by moving her? I didn't mean to hurt her,"

"How long?" the doctor asked again.

"I'm not sure. Five minutes, maybe less. I don't know for sure. Wait. It was immediately after calling 911," Tom said.

"The blow to her head knocked her out," said the doctor. "But, being face down in the dirt for over five minutes almost killed her. If you hadn't rolled her over when you did, she'd be dead right now."

"She's okay?" asked Big John.

"She should be. She has a huge hematoma on the back of her head and another one on her neck, along with a bunch of little cuts. We're concerned about some possible swelling of the brain. We're going to keep her for a few days and monitor her condition. She's also on oxygen to help with her breathing. You guys are really lucky. You could have lost your mother today. I'd say a prayer of thanks is in order, boys. I do believe God is watching over that woman."

"Thanks, doctor," said Tom.

"No reason for you to stay. I've given her pain medication and your mom is resting. She'll be out for some time. Go home. I'll call you if anything changes."

As Tom and Big John exited the hospital, Big John slapped Tom upside the head, making him yell.

"What did you do that for?" Tom said.

"Don't you ever hang up on me again," said Big John.

He slapped him again.

"What the fuck. What's wrong with you? What was that one for?" cried Tom

"Because, you're an idiot."

Seventeen

Dr. Wasserman monitored Melissa closely. She slept most of the time and was confused as to what had happened to her. Tests showed that she had some swelling of the brain tissue, probably due to the lack of oxygen. He decided to wait and see if the swelling would go down on its own before taking the next step, which would be surgery.

Now, twenty-four hours later, her three sons were with her in her hospital room. She knew they were there but she was too tired to open her eyes and speak.

"She looks terrible," said Tom. "I've never seen her look so bad."

"Well, you did drop a chainsaw on her head," replied Bobby. "What do you expect?"

"It was an accident," Tom responded. "I didn't do it on purpose. How many times do I have to tell you that?"

"Whatever," said Bobby. "But, if you were going to drop it, couldn't you have turned it on first."

Melissa almost opened her eyes when she heard that remark.

"I said I was sorry. Big John already gave me hell for what I did. I feel bad enough, so just let it go, will you?" snapped Tom.

That's my boy, thought Melissa. He's sorry for what happened. She opened her eyes just a crack and peaked at her three sons. Bobby was sitting in a guest chair and the other two were standing, facing the window.

They are good boys, she thought. Big John is so dark and has such beautiful big brown eyes. And, strong. They were all strong, but nobody messed with Big John. Sweet Bobby. Wait. Didn't he just make a smart-ass remark? I can't remember. Look at him, sitting there eating a candy bar. Someday he'll be fat. And, my baby Tom. He worries me, with him being so much like his daddy. No ambition, but he can charm the pants off a nun. His sweet smile has helped him out of a lot of messes. I sure do have a soft spot for that one.

I'm so tired, she thought. Then, the sound of the boys' voices slowly slipped away, as Melissa fell into a coma.

Dr. Wasserman was in the hospital waiting room, talking to the three boys. "It may last a couple of days, or it could be weeks. Some people never come out of a coma. I don't think that's going to happen with your mother. She will probably come out of this, but there's no way to actually tell."

"You don't know how long?" asked Big John.

"No way to know. Just be prepared for the worst and hope for the best. And, there is no guarantee that when she does wake up, she will be her old normal self."

"Why not?" inquired Tom.

"She may have some memory loss, slight brain damage, any number of things. We just need to wait and see," Dr. Wasserman replied. "Remember, she had severe trauma to her head. Most people would have been killed by a blow like that. How much does a chainsaw weigh? Eleven--twelve pounds? That's a lot of weight to fall thirty feet and hit you on the head."

"What can we do?" asked Tom.

"Best you just talk to her. No one is sure if a comatose patient can hear what you are saying, but the sound of a loved one's voice seems to help."

"Thanks, doctor," said Big John, as Dr. Wasserman stood and left the waiting room.

"Hear that, boys," said Tom. "We better watch what we say in front of mama. She might hear us."

Eighteen

Ten days had passed since Melissa had slipped into a coma and eight days since she had come out of it. The doctor told everyone it was rare for a coma to last only a couple of days and they should be grateful that their mom was awake. The hospital staff spent the next week working with Melissa. The first few days after she woke up, she was foggy with some details and had a little trouble with her balance. As the week went on, she returned to her normal self and, by the end of the week, the staff was more than ready to see her leave the hospital.

On the Wednesday before she left to go back home, Sheriff Jason "Cowboy" Berkson visited her in her hospital room and asked her about the accident.

"Do you remember what happened, Melissa? When strange things happen around here, like your accident, we need to make sure there wasn't no hanky panky going on."

"Cowboy, there wasn't any hanky panky going on. My Tom was cutting a big limb off that big old Bitternut Hickory growing in my front yard. When the branch broke off, it scared him and he dropped that saw. I moved, to get out of the way of the falling branch, and walked right under that falling chainsaw.

"Doc Wasserman tells me you've had a lot of accidents lately. What's going on with you, sweetie?"

"Don't you go calling me sweetie, Cowboy. You got a good wife at home. Don't you be starting that crap with me."

"Sorry. Guess I got carried away there for a minute. Always had a little crush on you, you know."

"I bet you a pig's knuckle that crush started about the same time I became rich," Melissa said laughing.

"Just might be, girl. Just might be," the sheriff said, smiling. "You take care and if you need anything, Melissa, you call me, hear?"

"Got it. Bye, Cowboy."

"It's absolutely beautiful. I think I'm going to cry," Melissa said, as she got out of Bobby's truck and looked at her trailer.

"Do you really like it, Mom?" said Bobby.

"It's exactly like I pictured it," she replied.

"We're just about done. The only things that are left to do are the sidewalk and the flowerbeds. We wanted to ask you where you want them and what kind of plants you have in mind. I thought we should make the sidewalk angle around from where we park and then to the front door. Makes no sense to go straight out to the road with it when we park over here now, does it?"

"Look at the grass. It's beautiful. No weeds or bare spots. And, the fence. What a beautiful blue picket fence. Oh, I just know I'm going cry."

"Now, Mama, you don't wanna do that. I'm just so glad you're so happy. It's good to have you back home, "Bobby told her.

"Did you miss me, Bobby?" Melissa asked.

"Well, I sure did miss your cooking. Just kidding. Sure, I missed you, but I did see you every day in the hospital."

"You visited me every day?" Melissa inquired.

"We all did, Mama. Every one of us visited you and talked to you. Every single day. We prayed, too. We prayed for you to get better."

The tears started rolling down Melissa's face, as she listened to her son. "I don't know what I ever did to deserve such wonderful boys," she said. "I'm truly blessed."

She was surprised at how clean the house was when she went inside. The dishes were washed, beds were made, and the carpet looked like it had just been vacuumed.

With little to do, Melissa took it easy for the next few days. She spent some time catching up on her emails, paid some bills, and watched a lot of TV. When the headaches were finally tolerable, she stopped the pain medication. She was beginning to feel like her old self.

The boys were more than aware that their old mom was back. Her complaining had reached its full level and nothing they did was good enough.

Melissa had made an appointment with an attorney. She

figured she had held off long enough and it was time to get her affairs in order. She didn't plan to die for a long time, but you just never knew when it might happen.

David Branson's office was in a strip mall just off Roark Valley Road in Branson. He was a good-looking man of around fifty or fifty-five, had dark brown hair with just a touch of gray, and piercing green eyes.

"Mrs. Johnson. So good to meet you," he said, as he shook her hand. "Please have a seat."

"Melissa, please. Everyone calls me Melissa."

"Melissa. You can call me David."

"You related to the Bransons that founded this town?" she asked.

"Shirttail relative. We go back a long way. So, what can I do for you today?"

"I need a Will," she said.

"That's simple enough. Do you also need a Living Will?" David asked.

"I've heard about those. Something about pulling the plug or not pulling it. Just what is it, exactly," Melissa responded.

"A Living Will gives instructions to the doctor and hospital if you are facing the end. It answers questions the doctor would normally ask your family and they have to decide on the answers. If you have a Living Will, it takes the pressure off the family, as the decisions were already been made by you. For example, do you want to be kept alive by machines or do you want to be fed through a tube? I have a list of questions that we'll go through and you make the decisions."

"What if I can't tell them? You know, like I'm in a coma or something."

"You appoint an executor to carry out your wishes. He has the power."

"I think that's a good idea. I can see where this can sure eliminate a lot of fighting," said Melissa.

"Especially when one family member thinks the doctor should pull the plug, so to speak, and another wants to keep their loved one alive, no matter what the circumstances. It's good to have one."

"So, let's write one of those, too."

"My fee is $250.00 per document," David told her.

"That's fine. Whatever you think I should have is fine with me. Should we get started?" Melissa asked.

Two hours later Melissa left his office with a smile on her face. The last thing he had asked her was if she would go to dinner with him.

Nineteen

Melissa walked into the living room and twirled. "How does your mama look, boys? Not bad for a woman pushing fifty, right?"

"Where you going all dolled up?" asked Tom.

"I have a date," Melissa told him.

"With who? A blind man," said Bobby.

"Shut up. I don't need your crap," retorted Melissa. "Where's Big John?"

"He's out back, hunting squirrels," said Tom.

"It's too dark to be hunting," said Melissa.

"Not that dark," replied Tom.

"I'm leaving. When you see Big John, tell him I want a family meeting tomorrow. There are some things we need to talk about. When are you planning on finishing up the yard?"

"We'll finish up the yard as soon as you tell us where you want those stupid flower beds," said Tom.

"I think Big John has plans for tomorrow," said Bobby. "I think he and Cynthia are driving to Springfield for some concert or something."

"A million shows to see right here in Branson and he has to go to Springfield to see a concert," Melissa said. "I don't get it."

"So, who's the lucky guy? Who you going out with?"

asked Tom.

"It's none of your business, but if you must know, it's David Branson. He's my lawyer. A very nice man."

"David Branson? We know all about David Branson, right Bobby?" said Tom.

"What could you possibly know about him?" asked Melissa.

"Mom, it's all over the news," said Tom. "A couple of women have come forward and accused him of date rape."

"I don't believe it," said Melissa. "He's such a nice man."

"I don't think you should go out with him," said Tom. "It's really not a good idea."

"Seriously, Mom, you should just call and cancel. You dating anybody isn't a good idea, anyway," said Bobby.

"Y'all just prefer it if I sat here night after night wasting away rather than have a little fun, wouldn't you? Well, I'm going out to dinner with him and that's final."

"Just watch your drink," said Bobby. "They found Rohypnol in a urine test they gave a woman when she reported him to the police. Of course, your boyfriend denied it was him who gave it to her."

"He's not my boyfriend. What is that? That Rohypnol stuff", she asked.

"It's a date rape drug. Makes you lose control so men can do whatever they want to you. Just be careful," said Bobby.

"I'm leaving," she said, as she picked up her purse and headed out the front door.

She practically bumped into Big John, who was coming up the steps.

"Where you going?" he asked her, as they passed each other.

"Out," she barked, "And don't try to stop me."

"What's wrong with her?" Big John said as he entered the living room.

"We were just giving her a bad time," said Tom.

"Ya," Bobby said, laughing. "She's got a date with David Branson and Tom just told her he was a date rapist."

"Are you fucking kidding me?" said Big John. "And, she believed it?"

"Think so," said Tom. "That should be one interesting date. I can just picture her now, sitting at the table, making sure he doesn't get within three feet of her drink."

"You know when she finds out you were lying, she's gonna kill you two," Big John said, laughing so hard he could hardly get the words out.

Melissa met David at Bowerfield's, an upscale restaurant by Branson Landing. He had arrived before her and was sitting at a table near a window.

"You look lovely," he said, as the maître d' showed her to the table.

"Thank you. You look very handsome tonight," she responded, as she sat down.

The waiter brought them menus and asked if they would like a cocktail before dinner. David ordered a dry martini and Melissa passed.

"You don't drink, Melissa?" he asked.

"Occasionally," she said. "But never when I'm driving."

"I could have picked you up, you know," he said.

"Yes, but then I'd be riding in a car with someone who is driving and who has been drinking. It's the same thing, don't you think?" she said.

David laughed. "Can't argue with that," he said.

The busboy filled their water glasses and Melissa immediately picked her glass up and took a large swallow.

"Are you alright?" David asked. "You seem nervous."

"A little, I guess," she replied. "To be honest, I don't date much. In fact, this is the first date I've had in a long time. I dated some after Joe left. However, a woman raising three little kids isn't exactly what most men are looking for. I was pretty busy working and taking care of the boys. Got out of the habit of having a man around and, after a while, I didn't miss it."

"Well, the ones who didn't ask you out are fools. I find you to be a fascinating woman."

"Seriously?" she laughed. "I'm anything but fascinating."

"I think it's fascinating that you are worth over seven

million dollars and you live in a trailer. Most people would have bought the most expensive house they could find if they inherited the kind of money you have."

"It's not a trailer," replied Melissa.

"Excuse me," said David.

"It's not a trailer. I don't live in a trailer. It's a mobile home."

"Alright. Why don't you buy a house? There's a lot of good real estate for sale around here."

"David, I may buy a new house. Maybe I won't. I doubt I will, but if I do, it's not going to happen soon. I like my home. I've spent twenty-seven years there. We've fixed up the yard and it's as pretty as any of those million-dollar joints around here. I don't think the value of your home makes you a better person. You can be a saint living in a dump or a date rapist living in a mansion. The value of my home is not who I am."

"I hit a nerve. I'm sorry. I didn't mean anything by that. I was just curious."

"As long as we're getting so personal, I have a question for you."

"Anything you want to know," David said.

"Is it true what they are saying about you?"

"What are they saying about me? And, who are they?" he said.

"About the rapes. Is it true that two women have

accused you of date rape?" she asked at the same time David decided to take a sip of his martini.

"Sorry," he said, as Melissa wiped some of his drink off her face with her napkin. "I didn't think I could be shocked anymore, but that did it. Where in the world did you hear that?"

"It's not true?"

"It's as far from the truth as you can get."

"Then, it's my turn to apologize. I'm sorry. I guess I heard some bad gossip. Seriously, David, I'm so sorry."

"I think someone's been pulling your leg and I have a pretty good idea who," he said.

"Do you handle criminal cases?" she asked. "Because I think I'm going to be arrested for murder."

"How'd the date go?" asked Bobby as Melissa walked in the front door.

"Fine." She snapped. "Just fine."

"What's the matter? Did your boyfriend get fresh with you?" Bobby said.

Melissa gave them a dirty look, walked into her bedroom, and slammed the door shut behind her.

Bobby looked at Tom and the two of them broke into laughter.

Twenty

Melissa was sitting at the kitchen table talking to her three sons. They had just finished eating a nice home-cooked meal and were relaxing.

"You sure are a good cook, Mom," said Big John. "I'm gonna miss your cooking when I move out. By the way, I found a place. Cynthia likes it and it's affordable. We plan to make an offer on Saturday. Is that twenty thousand still on the table?"

"Perhaps it is and perhaps it isn't. We'll get into that later. Right now, I want to talk about finishing up the outside. How much do you think you've spent so far?" Melissa asked.

"I lost track," said Tom.

"Of course, you did," replied Melissa.

"I figure about ten thousand," said Bobby.

"Bobby, the roof alone cost around five thousand. It's a lot more than that, right mama?" asked Big John.

"I added it all up. I might have missed a few little miscellaneous charges, but I figure it has cost around fourteen thousand dollars. It would have cost twice that much if you boys hadn't done the labor. I figure you saved me a lot of money.

"You said we could have anything under twenty thousand that we didn't spend," said Bobby.

"That's right," answered Melissa. "We still have the sidewalk to do, though. I'm thinking about that. And, the flowerbeds. Those won't cost much. Probably a couple hundred for some plants and little bushes. I don't want you boys to do the sidewalk. That should be done by a professional. So, right now, I'm calling it at fourteen thousand and I'll cover any other minor expenses."

"So, we get to keep the six thousand dollars? That's two thousand each," said Bobby.

"That's right," replied Melissa.

"What about the twenty thousand?" asked Bobby.

"I'm gonna gift Big John another twelve thousand," said Melissa. "I can gift fourteen thousand a year, tax-exempt, to each of you boys. So, Big John, that'll make fourteen, and the other six thousand I'll give to you right after the first of the year."

"That sounds fair," said Big John. "What about Tom and Bobby?"

"They each get two thousand. That's their share of the six thousand left from fixing up the yard. That should also be enough to pay for first and last months' rent with a little left over."

"Nooo! You can't do that. It's not fair. Why does Big John get all the money and we don't? I've done most of the work. I should get a bigger share than they get." Tom yelled.

"Mom?" said Bobby with a shocked look on his face.

"Mom, why are you doing this?"

"Don't like it, eh?" said Melissa. "Kinda feel like you've been punched in the gut?"

"Well, ya," answered Tom. "I feel sick. I was counting on that money."

"I guess that's how David Branson must have felt last night when I asked him about the rape accusations," said Melissa, as she got up from the table and walked out of the room.

While her three sons sat at the kitchen table in total silence, Melissa left the house and drove away.

"Where do you think she's going?" said Tom finally said.

"Who gives a shit," replied Bobby.

"This isn't good," said Bobby. "She's getting too much advice."

"I'm killing her. I mean it. I'm killin' that bitch," said Tom. "Big John, do you know if she's signed that Will yet?"

"She's signing it next week sometime," said Big John. "She told me yesterday that David Branson was getting all her legal stuff in order. He's drawing up her Will, a Living Will, Power of Attorney information and she's making him the executor of her estate." He started to chuckle and said, "Man, that joke sure came back to bite you guys in the ass."

"That's not funny, Big John. You get your twenty thousand. We get crap," said Tom. "What am I supposed to do now?"

"You could get a job," said Bobby.

"Fuck you, Bobby," Tom threw back at him.

"Ya, well, fuck you, too, Tom, This is all your fault," said Bobby.

"How's it my fault?"

"You're the one who said David Branson committed date rape."

"Ya, well, you played along. You're as much to blame as I am," Tom replied.

"Enough," said Big John. "Let's head over to Waxy's and have a beer and talk about this."

Waxy's was crowded, but they managed to find a table. They ordered and waited for their beers to be served.

"First, let's get one thing straight," said Big John to his two brothers, as soon as the beers arrived. "Nobody is killing mama."

"I'm not finishing the flower beds," said Tom. "I'm done breaking my back for that bitch."

"Tom. Focus," said Big John. "We're not talking about a couple of flower beds right now. This talk about killing mama has to stop. If someone overhears you or you even joke about it, and then something happens to mama, we're gonna be in deep shit. Understand, Tom?"

"She can't do that to us," Tom said. "It isn't fair."

"Okay. Loosen up. I wasn't supposed to tell you guys, but the thing is.... well, it's all a joke. She asked me to go along with her for a few days so you would suffer. But this talk about killing her has to end. Got it?" Big John said.

Tom and Bobby glared at Big John. "You son of a bitch," said Bobby. "You knew that was a joke and you sat there and let her do that to us? I oughta punch your lights out."

"You seriously want to try that?" Big John asked him.

"Wait. Are you telling us that we are going to get the twenty thousand? This was just a joke?" Tom inquired.

"You're not supposed to know. But, yes, it was all a joke. It was mama's way of getting even with you for what you said about David Branson. You can't let on that I told you."

"So, we get the money?" Tom asked.

"I don't know. She changes her mind from one day to the next. I think you are. I know I'm getting the twenty-thousand, just like she said. I guess that's right about being able to gift fourteen thousand a year to people, tax-free. I bought a house, so I know I'm getting mine. However, if she sticks to her guns, you boys aren't going to see more than that two thousand right now."

While the boys were at Waxy's drinking beer, Melissa was having a drink with David Branson at Slippery Jim's Bar.

"You actually told them that?" asked David. "You let

them believe you were cutting them off?"

"Sure did. Those two little brats need to suffer for what they said about you. They may just think twice before lying to me again."

"You sure are a tough mama," said David. "Remind me not to get on your bad side. I'd hate to think what would happen."

"They just need to learn not to lie to their mama," she said.

"Melissa, would you like to go on a cruise with me?" David asked, changing the subject.

"What? Slow down, boy. I've had one dinner with you and you want to take me on a cruise? You're moving a little fast, don't you think?

"Two dates. I'm considering this a date. Besides, the cruise isn't until November. By then, I plan on knowing you real well."

"I've never been on a cruise. I'm not comfortable being on the water. Never have been. I don't know how to swim. What if we sink?"

"Cruise ships very rarely sink. And, every passenger has a life jacket. So even if the ship did sink, which is highly unlikely, you would still be able to float."

"I don't know, David. I'll have to think about it."

"Don't think too long. I'll need to make reservations," he replied.

"I like your name. I've always loved the name David. I don't know why I didn't name one of my boys David. David was God's favorite, even though he sinned a lot. Are you a religious man, David?" Melissa asked him.

"I know my bible," he replied.

"Are you anything like God's David from the bible?

"How so?" he asked.

"You know. Mostly good, but sometimes bad."

"Aren't we all a little bad at times?" asked David. "What about you, Melissa? Are you ever bad?"

"You wanna find out just how bad I can be?" Melissa replied.

"I plan on it. Believe me, I can hardly wait to find out."

Twenty-one

The house was quiet for the next few weeks. The subject of money hadn't been brought up again. Both Tom and Bobby had apologized to Melissa for the joke they had played and she coldly accepted their apology. She did not apologize for what she had done.

Big John was spending most of his spare time with Cynthia. He was getting ready to close on the house he had bought and they were busy picking out furniture and houseware goods. Cynthia did not care much for Melissa and the two were not close. Melissa stayed out of their way and let them go about their business. Although she had been pushing the boys to move out, now that Big John was actually leaving, she was miserable. Her rock was leaving her.

Tom had finished the flowerbeds and they were ready for the plants. He had asked his mother a few times to pick out what she wanted, but she just ignored him. He gave up.

Bobby went about his business, going out most nights, leaving Tom alone. Melissa spent most of her evenings with David Branson.

Tom was home alone, watching TV, when he thought he heard a knock on the front door. He muted the TV and listened. He heard another knock and got up off the couch wondering who it could be this time of night. He turned on the porch light and looked through the window. A man, who he did not recognize, was standing there.

"What do you want?" he yelled through the door.

"Is your mother home?" the man said.

"What do you want her for?" Tom asked.

The man didn't answer. Tom reached over and grabbed the shotgun that was leaning against the wall. It was kept handy and loaded, mostly to scare off wild animals venturing too close to their property. The number of packs of dogs running wild in the area was increasing. And, they were always hungry.

"She's not home," he yelled.

"Which one are you?" the man said.

"Which one what?" replied Tom.

"Which kid are you?"

An hour later, when Melissa arrived home, she wondered who owned the strange car parked in front of the house. As she walked through the front door, she saw a man sitting on the couch talking to Tom.

"Hi, mom," said Tom. "Look who's here."

Disbelief showed on Melissa's face as she stared at the man. "Joe?" Melissa said.

"Hello, Missy. It's been a long time."

"Not long enough, you bastard," she yelled. "What the hell are you doing here? Tom, what's going on?"

"I wanted to meet my daddy," Tom said with a stupid grin on his face.

"Get out," she screamed. "Get out right now or I'm calling the police."

"Calm down, woman. You'll wake the dead with all that yelling. God! You haven't changed a bit. Well, actually you have. You got old and you've put on a few pounds. Looks like your face has had a rough time, too."

"Joe, shut the fuck up and get out of here right now," she said, trying to control herself. "There's no reason for you to be here and no reason for you to stay."

"I was just passing through and wanted to say hi. Word's out your daddy left you a bunch of money. I could sure use a little of that." Joe said.

Melissa was standing by the front door. She slowly reached over and pick up the shotgun.

"I have no problem shooting you right here, Joe. So, I think you better get your ass off that couch and get the hell out of here."

Joe looked at her and slowly got up from the couch. "You're still a bitch," he said. "I'm leaving, so just simmer down."

Melissa, still holding the shotgun, backed out of his way, and watched him head for the front door.

Joe turned around before he left and looked at Tom. "I sure enjoyed our visit, son. Maybe, I'll see you at your mama's funeral."

Melissa locked the door and put the gun down. "Why did you let him in here, Tom?"

"I wanted to meet my dad," he replied.

"That man is trouble. You stay away from him."

"He seems nice. I liked talking to him."

"Tom, when that man left us, it was the only good thing he ever did. He's no good."

"He told me he was gonna be in town for a few days. I just might see him again. You can't tell me what to do anymore."

"You've seen the scars on Big John's back, right?" Melissa asked.

"I've seen 'em. Big John won't talk about how he got them."

"Your wonderful father, who you might see again, did that to him when he was four years old. He beat him with a belt until he bled. Then he ran. He knew I would sic the police on him, so he took off. He was no good then and he's no good now."

"Did he hit you, too?" asked Tom.

"You don't need to know any more of this stuff. He's been out of our lives for over twenty-three years. Let's keep him out for another twenty-three."

"I guess. He sure doesn't like you, either." Tom said.

"For good reason."

"What's that?"

"Well, for starters," said Melissa, "Right before I kicked his ass out, I shot him."

"You did what?" Tom asked, surprised. "Where'd you shoot him?"

"You notice he's missing part of his right ear?"

"Ya, I noticed that," replied Tom.

"I did that," Melissa said.

"What did y......," Tom started to ask.

"No more." She interrupted. "No more talk about him. Just one thing, Tom. Are you the one who told him about me getting some of daddy's money?"

"No. He knew it when he got here. I didn't tell him."

Melissa smiled at her son. "I believe you. How about you and I go pick out some plants for those flowerbeds tomorrow?"

Twenty-two

Two weeks later, Big John moved out. Things had gotten back to normal and everybody was talking to each other again. The joking around was as lively as ever. Melissa cried a little when Big John moved, but he told her he would be over for dinner soon and she would see him then.

Bobby and Tom fought over who would get Big John's room. Both wanted it for their own, as it was the larger of the two rooms. Age won out and Bobby finally had his own room.

"I don't know why you are even bothering with it," Melissa said to them. "You're both going to be packing up and leaving in a few weeks. Seems silly to move stuff when you're going to be moving it again."

"I figure if I'm gonna be here for another month or so, I might as well enjoy it. I've been listening to him snore and fart long enough," said Bobby.

"Ya? Well, you aren't exactly a rose garden. I'll be glad to get away from your stink," replied Tom.

"You both stink," said Melissa.

"I got a job," said Tom.

Melissa and Bobby looked at him in shock. Tom hadn't worked in over two years.

Finally, Melissa said, "That's the best news I've heard in a long time. Where?"

"The Showboat Lilly Belle," he answered. "I'm going to be a server."

"I heard they make good money," said Bobby.

"It's seasonal," said Melissa. "That boat doesn't run all year."

"Wrong. It might slow down a little during the off-season, but it runs all year."

"When do you start?" asked Bobby.

"Pretty soon. I'm waiting for a call to tell me exactly when."

"Praise God," said Melissa. "Miracles do happen. I'm proud of you, Tom. It took a while to find a job, but you never gave up."

"I'm looking for a place to rent. I was wondering if I could stay here a little longer until I save some money."

"You should have enough with the money I gave you to get into an apartment," Melissa said.

"Well, it's like..... it's...... umm........." he stuttered.

"It's what?" asked Melissa.

"It's gone," he answered.

"It's gone? I just gave it to you. What could you have possibly spent two thousand dollars on?" his mother asked him.

"I didn't exactly spend it. I'm gonna get it back. I loaned it to someone," he answered.

"Oh, god, don't tell me. You gave it to Fat Joe, didn't

you? Did you give that money to your no-good father?"

"He really needed it. He said he couldn't leave town until he got his car fixed and he had to rent a motel room for a couple of nights. He's gonna pay me back."

"No, Tom. He isn't. You aren't gonna see a penny of that money from him, ever. He's a bum. This is the kind of crap he does. You might just as well of lit a fire and thrown that money into it to burn. It's gone, son," Melissa told him.

"What am I gonna do?" he whined. "I'm broke until I get a paycheck."

"Your problem," replied Melissa.

"Can I stay for a little while longer?" he asked.

"I'll think about it," answered Melissa.

"What about me?" asked Bobby. "Do I have to move out right away or can I stay as long as Tom?"

"Do you still have the money I gave you?" asked Melissa.

"Yes," he replied.

"Then you have to move out," she told him.

Twenty-three

"Bobby, come here,"

"What the hell, Tom? You scared me. I thought you were outside. What are you doing in Mom's bedroom?"

"Look what I found."

"What?"

"A copy of mom's Will," said Bobby.

"Put that away. Mom's gonna kill you if she catches you in here,"

"She's at the store. She won't be home for a couple of hours. Let's see what's in it."

"Put it away."

"Don't you want to see what's in it?" asked Bobby.

"Well, maybe just a peek. And, you better be sure you put it back exactly where you found it."

"I don't know. Fifty thousand isn't very much for what you want me to do," Hook said.

"Take it or leave it,"

"Let me think about it. I'm taking all the risk. If someone sees me or if I'm caught, I'll spend the rest of my life in jail. Or, worse."

"If you're careful, you won't get caught."

"Call me later and I'll give you an answer," Hook told him.

"No, you call me at this number. It's a burner phone. I

don't want your phone number being traced back to me."

Deer hunting season in Texas starts in early November and ends sometime in January, depending on which county of Texas you're hunting. Melissa's three boys had made deer hunting in Texas an annual affair.

For the past four years, they had taken their vacations at the beginning of November and headed to Texas. This year was no different and the plans were in the works. They were gathered around Melissa's kitchen table, making a list of what camping gear and supplies they needed to take with them.

"I'm gonna miss you three," said Melissa.

"Oh, ma, you say that every year. You're always sad when we leave, but I think you like being alone for a few days," said Bobby.

"Well, this will be good practice. Pretty soon, all of you will be gone and I'll be alone for good. Anyway, I'm leaving the day after you get back."

"Where you going?" asked Big John.

"I told you. I'm going on a cruise with David."

"I forgot. Have you learned to swim yet?" Big John asked. "What if the ship capsizes?"

"I'll have a life jacket on," Melissa said. "Everyone has to wear a life jacket while they are on the boat."

"Not exactly," said Bobby, laughing.

"David said everyone has a life jacket."

"Well, there are enough life jackets for the passengers. However, you don't wear them all the time. You wear them if there is an emergency, like hitting an iceberg," said Bobby.

"There aren't icebergs that far south. There aren't, are there, Big John?" she asked.

"No, mom. You don't have to worry about icebergs," he said. "Just sharks."

"You boys stop it. I'm nervous enough about being in the middle of the ocean. You don't have to make it worse."

The boys laughed and went back to concentrating on the plans for their trip. They told Tom they would help him out with his share of expenses. He could pay them back when he was working steady hours at the Showboat. So far, the job was only part-time and filling in when extra help was needed.

The next day, Big John came by the house to pick up Tom and Bobby. They loaded his truck with their supplies and piled in, as excited as little kids at Christmas. Melissa smiled. Every year she watched as they went through the same ritual and they were as excited now as they had been the first year.

She waved goodbye and watched them drive down the road. She gave a big sigh and headed back into the house. She was always a little sad when they left.

She needed to take a shower and get moving. She was

driving up to Springfield to do some shopping. It was a little late in the season to be buying cruise clothes, but she could probably find what she needed in a store there.

I'm going to buy everything I see that I want, she thought. David had told her that the passengers didn't get as dressed up as they did years ago, but she still wanted to look fashionable for him.

An hour later, Melissa locked the front door and headed to her car. As she walked by one of her flowerbeds, she bent to deadhead a bloom from a coneflower plant and heard a whizzing sound pass over her head. She also heard the klunk, as a bullet tore through the siding of her trailer, left a trail mark across her kitchen table, and came to a stop in her refrigerator door. Melissa hit the ground and froze. Someone had shot at her.

She stayed still for a couple of seconds, trying to decide if she should run to her car, or try for the house. A second shot missed directly hitting her but ricocheted off a large rock and hit her foot.

Melissa didn't move. Her foot was starting to burn and the inside of her shoe felt sticky. Suddenly, she heard car tires squeal and a big black car went roaring past her house. She glanced up, but couldn't see who was driving the car.

When she pulled off her shoe, her bloody little toe fell out and landed on the ground next to her.

"Shit," she moaned. "That really hurts."

Melissa picked up her toe, stood up, and hobbled back up the stairs and into the house, leaving a trail of blood behind her. She wrapped her foot in some towels and called 911.

"There's no way I'm going to be able to go," she said. "I'm gonna be in here for another day and probably on crutches for a few weeks.

Melissa was sitting up in her hospital bed talking to David.

"Then I'm not going either. The whole idea of us going on this cruise was to spend time alone and relax."

"Why don't you take your daughter or one of your grandkids? Seriously, David, it would be a shame to waste that money and not go. Don't worry about me. I'll be fine."

"I don't think I should leave you alone when there is someone out there trying to kill you," he replied. "It wouldn't be right."

"The boys will be home in a couple of days. I won't be alone. Tom and Bobby will be there."

Sheriff "Cowboy" Berkson stood in the hallway outside of Melissa's room and watched as Melissa and David talked. He wouldn't have any reason to hurt her, the sheriff thought. It looks like they are getting along just fine.

The sheriff entered Melissa's room and smiled. "You

sure do keep this hospital busy," he said laughing. "How's the foot?"

"It seems my little toe won't be going wee, wee, all the way home, anymore," said Melissa.

"Gone?" said the Sheriff.

"Yup," Melissa answered. "I'm just lucky it was only the toe. I could be dead right now if that guy was a better shot."

"You sure it was a guy?" he asked.

"No. I'm not sure about anything right now. I have no idea who it was. All I know is that they were driving a big black car. I can't even tell you the make. I was on the ground. You check out the house?"

"Yup. Casey took a bullet out of your refrigerator door. Same caliber as what took your toe off. I've got my men going through the woods across from your trailer. Doubt they'll find anything, though. The brush is really thick over there."

"It's not a trailer," said David, with a grin on his face.

Melissa ignored him and the remark. "My refrigerator got shot? I missed that when I went into the house. I've been meaning to replace that old thing anyway, so no great loss."

"It's not dead, Melissa," the sheriff said. "It's still working except now it's working with a hole in the door."

"I know it's not dead. What? You think I'm stupid?" she asked him.

"So, who have you pissed off lately?" the sheriff

continued.

"I know for sure it wasn't one of the boys. They are all in Texas hunting. Fat Joe showed up at my house a couple of weeks ago. I sent his ass flying. I thought he left town, though."

"He did. That doesn't mean he didn't sneak back in," said the sheriff. "I'll check that out. Anyone else you can think of? Anyone, besides the boys, who would have anything to gain if you were dead?"

"Not that I can think of," Melissa said.

"You going home tomorrow?" the sheriff asked. "I don't want you staying alone out there. You got anybody you can stay with?"

"I'll stay with her until the boys get back," said David. "I'm not about to leave her alone."

"You don't need to do that. I can take care of myself," she said.

"If you could, you wouldn't be here sitting on that bed," chuckled the sheriff.

Twenty-four

Melissa didn't feel safe in her own home and it pissed her off. Your home is the one place you should always feel safe. Now, some bastard had taken that away from her.

David had brought her home from the hospital and helped her get settled. He had a client he had to meet at the office and told her he would be back in a couple of hours. She was starting to rethink her decision about telling the boys they had to move out. Keeping Tom and Bobby around, at least until they found out who shot her, might be a good idea.

She experimented walking with crutches and found it easier if she only used one. She checked the shotgun behind the front door and made sure it was loaded. Then, she hobbled to her bedroom closet and took down a box, which held a Colt Defender .45 and a gun cleaning kit.

Melissa spent the next hour taking the pistol apart and carefully cleaning it. After she had re-assembled it and inserted the loaded clip, she slowly limped into the living room. She opened the door to the back steps that overlooked the woods and went outside. She focused on a big oak tree about seventy-five yards away and started shooting.

Not bad, she thought. She reloaded the gun and aimed at a closer tree. She emptied the clip and could see that the hits on the trunk of the tree were in a nice cluster. I'm ready, she thought. Wherever I go, so does this gun.

David spent the next few nights with her, catering to her every need. She felt a little embarrassed by all the attention, yet it also made her feel good to have someone take care of her.

Melissa had not called her sons and told them about the shooting. She figured there was nothing they could do, and she didn't want them cutting their trip short.

Now, they were back home. She watched as they pulled up to the trailer and got out of the truck. As she stepped out onto the porch to greet them, Bobby started laughing and the teasing started.

"Whatcha do now, mom?" Bobby asked. "Shoot yourself in the foot?"

"You might want to take it easy on your mom, boys," David said. "She's carrying."

"You leaving?" Melissa asked him.

"I'll call you later to make sure you're okay," he said, kissed her on the cheek, got in his car, and drove away.

"What did you do?" Big John asked her, now being serious. "What happened?"

"Somebody shot my little toe off," she said. "Good to have you back."

She glanced over at Tom who was looking a little sick and was still standing by Big John's truck watching her.

"Come on over here, Tom, and give your mama a kiss hello. You been carsick? You don't look so good."

"Tom. Bobby. You two get your stuff out of the truck. I'm gonna talk to mama for a minute before I leave," Big John told them.

"Did you get a deer?" Melissa asked as she hobbled back into the house and sat down at the kitchen table. "Want a beer?"

Big John opened the refrigerator, took out a cold beer, and asked, "Why is there a hole in the refrigerator door?"

"Someone tried to kill me. Took out the door and I'm minus one pinky toe," Melissa stated factually.

"Do you know who?"

"I know who it wasn't. Wasn't any of you boys. Other than that, the Sheriff doesn't have a clue," she answered.

"When did it happen?"

"The day you left," she responded.

She could see Big John try to control his temper as he asked the next question. "And, you didn't call us – why?"

"Because, I love you. There was nothing you could do and I didn't see any point in ruining your vacation. You boys wait all year for that trip and you, especially you, deserve to have some fun. So, don't be getting all huffy with me. I'm fine."

"You don't seem fine. Were you alone all the time we were gone?" Big John asked.

"After I got out of the hospital, David took care of me. I wasn't alone at night."

"What about your trip? You're not going, are you?"

"I'm not going. David is. He's taking his grandson, Joey. No sense in wasting a good vacation just because of me."

"I know I never tell you this, Mom, but if anything would ever happen to you, it would kill me. I can't imagine my life without you in it."

Melissa looked him in the eyes and smiled. "I love you, too, sweetie. Don't worry. I don't plan on going anywhere for a long time."

Bobby and Tom came into the house and deposited their camping gear and rifles in their rooms. As they walked by Melissa and Big John, Bobby said, "Open us a cold one, Big John. We gotta sit down and hear mama's toe story."

The three boys were quiet and didn't interrupt Melissa as she told them the details about the shooting. No one was joking now.

"You can't be alone," said Bobby. "From now on you have to be with one of us all the time."

"That's not practical or possible," said Melissa. "Now that I know someone might be trying to hurt me, I'll be on my guard. I've got my gun and I'm keeping it near me. I'm more likely to kill whoever is trying to kill me. That person certainly was a bad shot."

"Maybe it was a drive-by shooting," said Tom.

Melissa realized that this was the first time Tom had said anything since they had come back home. "Are you okay, Tom? You really don't look well,"

"I'm okay. I guess I was just shocked to see you standing there like that when we got home. I can't believe anyone would do that to you. I mean, like--I don't know. Someone tried to kill you, for god's sake, and you act like it's an everyday occurrence. How, can you be so cool about it?" he replied.

"Oh, baby, I'm not cool with this at all. If I ever find out who did this, I'm gonna skin 'em alive and then feed 'em to a pack of wild dogs. Believe me. I am not cool about this."

"Are you seeing David tonight?" Big John asked her.

"No, he's leaving early in the morning and has a bunch of stuff to do to get ready," his mother said.

Big John stood up. "I gotta go, Mom, but I'll check on you later."

"As for you two," he continued, "You better be sure one of you is with mama tonight. If anything happens to her, I'll take it out on your hides. Tom, walk with me, will you?"

Tom followed Big John outside and walked to his truck with him. "You sure seem upset over this," Tom said.

Big John grabbed Tom by the front of his shirt and pulled him up, his toes almost off the ground. "Listen to me. We talked some shit when mama first came into that money. All that talk about killing her was stupid talk. Just think if somebody had overheard us and now this happens to her. We'd be the first ones they'd suspect. You just better be sure you haven't done anything stupid because if I find out you were behind this – well, let's just say, they'll never find your body."

Tom pushed away from him. "When did you become so high and mighty? Getting rid of her was your idea in the first place."

"Just words, Tom. None of us was thinking straight when we first saw all those dollar signs. That was months ago. It's time you grew up. Mom worked like a dog all her life to take care of us and that's something none of us should ever forget. My god, she's still taking care of you. You should be grateful."

"You think I was behind this? You're wrong. This wasn't me. Sure, I've thought about it. We all have. But I could never hurt her."

"Just watch yourself," said Big John.

"Of course, you might change your mind if you knew what was in her Will," Tom retorted.

"I don't care what's in her Will. I'm warning you, Tom."

"Warn all you want, asshole."

As Tom turned and walked away from his big brother, he yelled back at him and said, "By the way, did you know I met our father?"

Twenty-five

Big John was furious. He couldn't prove that Tom had anything to do with the shooting, yet his gut told him that his brother was up to no good. He made a detour on his way home, drove into Hollister, and stopped at the police station.

Sheriff Berkson was sitting behind his desk, feet up, reading the newspaper.

"Hey, there, Big John. What can I do for you?"

"Got a minute, Cowboy?" he asked the sheriff.

"What do you need?"

"It's about mama. Do you have any idea who could have taken a shot at her?"

"Not a clue. It could have been random, but I don't think so. I think someone was sitting in those woods, across from her trailer, waiting for her to show herself."

"Mobile home," said Big John.

"What?"

"Never mind," answered Big John. "Do you know that Fat Joe was in town?"

"Your mom mentioned it. He was around for a couple of days and then gone. No one has seen him lately. We checked that out. Why? You think he might be behind this?" asked the sheriff.

"Don't know. I just heard a few minutes ago that he had been sniffing around. Just seems strange that he shows up and then someone tries to kill mom."

"How was the hunting? Kill anything?"

"We all got our bucks. Should be good eating. Well, I gotta get home. Thanks, Cowboy. Let me know if you hear anything."

"Sure will, Big John. Take it easy now, y'hear?"

"You were supposed to kill her, not shoot her toe off."

"She ducked. It was as if she knew a bullet was coming at her and she just ducked out of the way," Hook said.

"She bent down to pick a dead flower, you idiot. She isn't psychic and can tell when someone is going to shoot at her."

"I told you I wasn't great with a gun. And, don't call me an idiot," said Hook.

"Sorry. Anyway, you know what to do next?"

"I know," Hook replied.

"Let's go through it one more time."

"I know what to do. I've been drunk half my life. I don't need lessons on how to act."

"You know what to say? It has to be believable, Hook."

"Trust me. This I can do, no problemo," Hook replied.

"Are you gonna be able to handle the jail time?"

"You're kidding, right? Acting crazy for a few months, while having a place to sleep and free food, is a breeze. Like I said, no problemo."

"I'll contact you when it's time."

"You should give me something now," Hook said.

"I'm broke. You'll have to wait, just like the rest of us."

Two weeks later, Bobby moved out of his mother's trailer and into an apartment. Tom asked him if he could move in with him and Bobby told him no. "It's time for me to have my own place, Tom. I wouldn't be doing you any favors by letting you move in with me. You need to learn to take care of yourself."

Tom was fuming. The way he saw it, his brothers had left him to take care of his mother, while they were off doing their own thing. Everything had changed and he didn't like it one bit. He was almost twenty-four and, according to his mother's Will, he wouldn't see a penny of her money until he was thirty. He didn't want to wait six more years.

Friday nights were the busiest at BJ's Sports Bar. The tables were always full and the crowds were usually three deep at the bar. Tonight was no exception. Tom was standing at the bar enjoying his third beer. He turned and looked the crowd over and noticed Big John and Cynthia sitting at a table. Then, he saw Bobby walk through the entrance and go over and sit down with them. He picked up his beer and walked over to the table.

"Hi, bros. Room for one more?" he asked his brothers,

as he pulled up a chair and sat down.

"Where'd you come from?" asked Big John.

"I was over at the bar. Just noticed you guys," answered Tom.

"How you been, Tom? Haven't seen you for a while," asked Bobby.

"I've been working a lot. Listen, I'm sorry. Bobby, I was totally out of line getting ticked off like that. You were right. It is time I started looking out for myself. Big John, I'm sorry about our little misunderstanding. I really mean it. I hope we can just put it behind us. Hey, we're the three musketeers, right? We fight the bad guys, not each other. Right guys?"

"No sweat," said Bobby. "We're cool."

"What about mom?" asked Big John.

"What about her?" replied Tom.

"You have any more plans regarding her?"

"Big John, that wasn't me. I didn't have anything to do with mom getting shot. You gotta believe me. I was just running off at the mouth. We all did. I just took it too far. You haven't got anything to worry about from me."

"Well... I guess I believe you," Big John said. After a moment's hesitation, he smiled at Tom and said, "Okay, we're good. How about another beer?"

"You know me," said Tom. "I never turn down a free one."

Twenty-Six

Two days before Thanksgiving, at 12:52 am, the phone rang at the Hollister Police Department. Casey, who was working the night shift, answered it.

"Hollister Police Department. State your business."

"Is that you, Casey," asked Tom.

"Who's this?" Casey asked.

"It's Tom. Tom Johnson. Up here off Harper Lane."

"Sure. Melissa's boy. You need something?"

"You better get up here. I just got home and found mama. She's dead, Casey. My mama's dead."

"You sure this time, Tom?"

"That's not funny."

"Sorry. You call an ambulance, Tom? Casey asked.

"No need. Nothing they can do."

"I'll be right there. Don't touch anything," Casey told him, hung up, and dialed Sheriff Berkson. The sheriff told him to call the coroner and then head up to the trailer.

"There are definite signs of a struggle," said Sheriff Berkson. "She put up one hell of a fight."

"She kept a gun next to her bed," said Casey.

"Too bad she didn't get a chance to use it. There's a shotgun by the front door. I think if she heard a noise, she would have grabbed a gun. Whoever did this was quiet."

"The back door has been jimmied. Looks like that's

where they came in,"

"Or, made to look that way."

"What are you thinking, sheriff?" Casey asked.

"I'm thinking we need to find out where all her boys were tonight. I'm gonna go question Tom. Tell the coroner he can take Melissa when he's done here. I want to know the exact time of death asap."

Tom was sitting outside on the front steps, with his head in his hands and tears rolling down his cheeks.

"You're shaking, Tom. You cold?" asked the sheriff. "Or scared?

"Nothing for me to be scared about," Tom replied.

"You want to tell me what happened?"

"What's to tell? I came home and found mama like that. Lying half off the bed. I couldn't find a pulse and she felt cold. I called you. That's it," Tom told him.

"Where were you tonight?" Sheriff Berkson asked him.

"I met a few friends at a bar in Kirbyville and we spent the night bullshitting each other."

Just as the sheriff was about to ask Tom another question, a pickup truck came to a screeching stop in front of the trailer. Big John jumped out and ran towards Tom.

"What the hell did you do, Tom? What'd you do to mama?" he screamed. "I'm gonna fucking kill you."

Sheriff Berkson stepped in front of Tom. "Hold it right there, Big John. Nobody knows nothing, yet. Why are you flying off the handle at your brother?"

"God, Big John," said Tom. "Take it easy. I didn't do anything. I found her like that."

"Why are you blaming your brother? You know something you should tell me?" asked the Sheriff.

Big John took a step back, stumbling, and almost fell to his knees. "Is she really dead, Sheriff?"

"I'm sorry for your loss," the Sheriff replied, and Big John lost it.

The coroner was bringing Melissa's body out of the trailer when Bobby drove up and got out of his truck. He slowly walked to his brothers and nodded hello. The three sons watched as the coroner deposited their mother into the back of his van and drove away.

"I can't let you go inside. Tom, you'll have to find some other place to sleep tonight. It's late and I think you boys best leave now and go home. I've got work to do here. I'll talk to y'all tomorrow," the sheriff said.

"Do you know anything?" Bobby asked. "Was it a robbery gone bad?"

"Son," said the sheriff. "We've got a lot of questions that are going to need answering. Right now, you just need to go on back home and let us do our job. You'll know when we know."

"I can't believe this. Why would someone break in and smother her?" said Bobby. "It doesn't make any sense. She doesn't have anything worth stealing."

"Your mama was a rich woman," said the sheriff. "Maybe somebody thought she kept a lot of money here."

Casey and the sheriff were standing in the living room talking. "If this was a robbery, they sure were neat. Doesn't look like very much has been disturbed," said Casey.

"You're right. A few open drawers here and there and the guns left behind. You would have thought they would have been taken if somebody was robbing the place," said the sheriff.

"Staged, if you ask me," said Casey. "This wasn't a robbery gone bad. This was out-and-out murder."

"You may be right. And, I think Melissa knew her killer," the sheriff commented.

Twenty-Seven

The next morning Sheriff Berkson questioned Melissa's three sons. As far as he was concerned, they were all suspects. He started with Tom, who told him the same story as he had the night before.

"Who were these friends you met for a drink?" he asked Tom.

"Skinny Peterson and Jake Easley. I went to high school with them," Tom replied.

"I know 'em," said the sheriff. "What time did you get to the bar?"

"Around seven-thirty or eight," Tom answered.

"What time did you leave?"

"Around midnight," said Tom. "I'm pretty sure it was right around then. I had a lot to drink by then and I wasn't paying much attention to the clock."

"Four hours of drinking? Did you go straight home or stop off any place?"

"Drove straight home and then I found mama," Tom answered, his eyes starting to fill with tears.

"Took you almost an hour to get home from Kirbyville? That seems a long time for a short drive."

"I'd been drinking. It was dark and you know what those winding roads are like. I was careful, that's all. I took my time," Tom answered.

"Right. Who did you call after you found your mama?"

"I called you. Then I called Big John."

"You didn't call Bobby?"

"No."

"Anyone else?"

"No."

"I need your cell phone."

"No way. I need it."

"Tom," the sheriff said, "I'm not asking you. Give me your phone."

Tom reached into his back pocket, pulled out his phone, and threw it on the sheriff's desk.

"We done?" he asked him.

"For now, Tom. But, stick around. I might have more questions to ask you."

That one has a real fast temper, thought the sheriff, as Tom walked out of his office.

"I was in bed sleeping when Tom called," said Big John.

"Alone?" asked the sheriff.

"No. Cynthia was with me. You can ask her."

"I plan to. What time did Tom call?"

"It was a little after one. I'm not sure exactly how much. As soon as I heard him say that mama was dead, I threw on my jeans and drove straight to the house."

"What exactly did he say to you?" the sheriff asked.

"He said, 'John, I just got home and found mama and somebody killed her. She's dead. I've called the police. Get over here as fast as you can.' Or, words to that effect."

"Tom called you John? Not Big John?"

"I knew when he called me John that he was in trouble. The only time he calls me that is when he needs me to come help get him out of a mess."

"Then you called Bobby?"

"I did. I called him from my truck while I was driving over to mom's."

"What did you say to him?"

"I told him that Tom said mom was dead and he should get his ass over to the house," Big John said.

"Did you tell Bobby how your mother had been murdered?" asked the sheriff.

"I didn't know then. All I knew was that she was dead. It wasn't until I got to the house that I found out someone had smothered her."

"Who told you when you got to the house?" the sheriff inquired.

"You did."

"No, I didn't."

"Well, somebody did. I remember somebody saying it."

"I need to take a look at your phone, Big John."

Big John stood up, took his phone out of his back pocket, and handed it to him.

"Did you check out David Branson, sheriff? Maybe they had a fight or something and he's involved," Big John commented.

"How long, exactly, did your mom and David date?" the sheriff asked.

"I'm not totally sure. A few months, I guess. I know they were going together when mom got shot in the foot."

"Ya, I saw him with her at the hospital. I'll check him out, Big John. Thanks."

"Where were you last night, Bobby?" the sheriff asked.

"Nowhere," Bobby said. "I stayed home last night and watched TV."

"All night?"

"No, not all night. Earlier, I went to Walmart and did some grocery shopping. I was home by six-thirty, though. Never left the house until Big John called me."

"So, you were alone from six-thirty on?"

"No. I met a neighbor in the hall and asked him if he wanted to stop over for a beer."

"What time was that?" asked the sheriff.

"Right around six-thirty. It was when I got home from grocery shopping."

"Did he have a beer with you?"

"Ya. He came over around seven after I put my groceries away. We had a couple of beers and watched a little TV. He left early. Said he had to get back to his wife."

"What's his name?"

"Jason."

"Jason, what?"

"Fre...no, Foley. His name is Jason Foley."

"What time did he leave your place?" the sheriff asked.

"About eight. I don't think he stayed more than an hour."

"You got your phone on you?

"Ya, why?"

"I'm gonna need to take a look at it."

"That's it?"

"You can go. Oh, Bobby, one more thing. Who told you your mother had been smothered to death?"

"I think it was Tom."

"I didn't know Tom called you. I thought it was Big John."

"That's right, it was Big John," replied Bobby. "He told me when he called."

When the sheriff finished talking to them, he sent them home and told them not to leave town. Tom asked if he could go back home and the Sheriff told him he could as soon as the CSI finished with the trailer.

Mobile home, Bobby thought to himself. It seems strange that I'll never hear her say that again. She sure did hate it when you called her trailer a trailer.

Twenty-Eight

Sheriff Berkson spent the next twenty-four hours confirming alibis.

David Branson had been at a convention in Las Vegas at the time of the murder. A couple of thousand attorneys were his alibi. The sheriff hadn't thought he was involved, but you needed to check every lead you had.

Tom's friends said he had been with them, and in their sight, that night from about eight around midnight.

Cynthia confirmed that Big John and she went to bed around ten. She didn't hear Big John's phone ring, but she faintly remembered that, at some time during the night, he got out of bed.

Bobby was the sheriff's biggest concern. Jason Foley said he had spent about an hour with him between seven and eight. However, no one could confirm he was at home for the rest of the evening. Casey had asked the residents living at the apartment complex if they had seen Bobby leave at any time during the evening. Mrs. Joyce Skoup, an elderly woman whose apartment overlooked the parking lot, said Bobby's truck never moved after six-thirty. She was sure because she could see it from her window. "Besides," she told the sheriff, "If I'm asleep when he leaves or comes home, it makes so damn much noise, it wakes me up."

The sheriff had the cell phones checked and the findings

agreed with what the boys had told him. The night of the murder, Tom had called the sheriff and Big John and Big John had called Bobby. Tom had not called Bobby.

The coroner sent his findings to the sheriff, which only confirmed his suspicion of the cause of death, which was asphyxiation. She had been smothered to death. The coroner put the time of death somewhere between 9:30 p.m. and 11:30 p.m.

That meant Tom was in the clear unless his friends were covering for him. Big John was home in bed with Cynthia at that time. It looked like Bobby was the only one who didn't have a solid alibi.

Thanksgiving Day was a slow one for Sheriff Bergson. Most of the stores and bars were closed for the holiday, which cut down on the amount of traffic. He anticipated that the only calls he would go on would be to arrest some husband, who had drunk too much and was taking his anger out on his family.

The sheriff's wife said she would fix a couple of plates of food and drop them off for him and Casey. He loved turkey, but he was really looking forward to his wife's homemade pumpkin pie. She grew the pumpkins herself and every fall she canned a dozen or so jars of pumpkin.

Casey was dozing and nearly fell out of his chair when the phone rang, waking him up. The sheriff laughed and answered the call.

Casey listened to the one-sided conversation with interest. Sounded to him like he'd be going out.

"It's who? Crap. How long has he been there? He did what? Can he walk or is he too drunk? No, you don't have to wait around. I'm sending Casey right now. Thanks for calling."

The sheriff gave Casey a shit-eating grin and said, "That was Sammy. You need to go pick up Hook. He's over by the drugstore, lying on the ground, drunk as a skunk - again. Take the plastic sheeting to put over the back seat of the squad car. He threw up and Sammy says he stinks like crazy."

"Happy Thanksgiving to you, too," said Casey, as he headed out the door.

A half-hour later, Casey walked in with Steve Salitor, aka Hook, and locked him in a cell. Hook was around forty-five years of age but looked at least sixty. He wasn't exactly the town drunk. He was more like the town's part-time drunk. He would go for months without a drink and then he'd fall off the wagon. He worked when he was sober, doing odd jobs around town. He didn't make a lot of money, but he always had enough to buy a drink.

"You need to listen to what that crazy old drunk is mumbling about," Casey said to the sheriff.

"He can hardly walk much less talk and make any sense," replied the sheriff.

"He was talking about Melissa. Said something about her being psychic and knowing when bullets fly. Some crap like that."

"What are you talking about?"

"Sheriff, he mumbled all the way back here. He said stuff like getting even with some kid for not getting paid, it wasn't his fault that she ducked. Crazy stuff, I know. But I think he knows something about Melissa."

"Son of a bitch," said the sheriff. "We may have just found out who shot Melissa. Put on a pot of coffee. We're gonna sober up that old fart."

It took two pots, but an hour later Hook, who was still half-drunk, was talking. The sheriff promised him he wouldn't go to jail if he told him everything and Hook spilled his guts.

Before he even finished telling the sheriff how he had tried to kill Melissa, Casey had already headed out to pick up Tom. Now, the sheriff just had to figure out how Tom had managed to kill his mother.

"You can't possibly believe that old drunk," Tom complained to the sheriff. "I loved my mother. Why would I want her dead? That's crazy. This is a big mistake. Hook is lying. I don't even know him."

"He sure knows you, Tom. He does seem a little put out that you didn't pay him for the job."

"What job? There was no job. Seriously, Cowboy, you gotta believe me."

"Funny thing, Tom. I'm leaning more toward believing Hook. I've already checked the security tapes from the restaurant where you two met. I have you chatting away with him on tape. Before and after he shot at your mom."

"You're wrong. That isn't me," Tom argued.

"Tom, I'm arresting you for attempted murder. I thank the good Lord that your mother isn't around to see this. Who'd you hire to kill her? Why don't you save me some time and just confess?"

"I didn't fucking kill her. You can't pin that on me. I have witnesses where I was."

"I wonder how much you promised to pay Skinny and Jake if they lied for you. Too bad, they're never going see that money."

"They didn't lie. I didn't do it," Tom yelled. "I didn't smother my mother."

"Casey," the sheriff said, "Read him his rights and lock him up."

Casey walked Tom to the back of the jail and put him in a cell next to Hook.

Casey walked back to his desk and sat down. The sheriff told him, "I just called the manager of that restaurant where

Hook says he met with Tom. He checked to see if he has the security tapes from that night. No luck. The security camera hasn't worked for a couple of months."

"Are you really letting Hook off the hook?" Casey asked.

"Hell, no. That bastard tried to kill Melissa. That's attempted murder. His attorney will argue we coerced him while he was drunk and he didn't know what he was saying. Drunk or not, we have his confession on tape. Neither one of those pricks are going anywhere."

"You want me to turn the mic on so we can hear what those two are talking about back there?" asked Casey.

"I think Hook passed out. And, I don't feel like spending the rest of my shift sitting here listening to Tom cry," said the sheriff, laughing.

Twenty-nine

Bobby was sitting in a recliner in Big John's living room, having a beer with his brother.

"Can you believe Tom hired Hook to shoot mom?" he said.

"Ya, I believe it," said Big John. "Ever since she came into all that money, all he's talked about is getting rid of her. I didn't think he'd be so stupid as to try to hire someone, though. And, he picks Hook, who is definitely not the brightest bulb on the tree. That was stupid hiring stupid to do something stupid."

"That's funny," said Bobby. "Stupid hiring stupid to do something stupid. I gotta remember that."

"We gotta plan mom's funeral," said Big John. "The sheriff said they'll release the body as soon as the autopsy results come back."

"I thought they knew everything. What else do they need?" asked Bobby.

"They run tests to check for different drugs in her body. I guess all the results haven't come back yet. Bobby, do you think Tom had mom killed?" Big John asked.

"Honestly, I don't have a clue. He has a solid alibi, which is more than I have. I guess if he hired someone to shoot her, he could have hired someone to smother her."

"Did Tom tell you that Fat Joe had been out to the

trailer?"

"What? When did that happen?" asked Bobby.

"A few weeks back. Mom came home while he was there and threw a fit. Kicked his ass right out the door."

"What if Fat Joe killed mom?" asked Bobby.

"What if Tom hired Fat Joe to kill mom?" Big John asked him back.

"I wonder if the sheriff is looking for him. I've gotta give him a call."

"How about we just stop over and visit Tom and ask the sheriff when we get there? Right now, we have to plan a funeral."

When Big John and Bobby walked into the police station, Casey was sitting at his desk, feet up, reading a newspaper, As soon as he saw them, he leaned over and flipped a switch, which turned off the mic. No need, he figured, that anyone to find out that the sheriff had bugged the jail cells so they could listen to the prisoners' conversations.

"What can I do for you boys? Here to see your brother?" he asked.

"We brought him a chicken dinner if that's okay with you. Figure he's probably hungry," said Bobby.

"Why, boys, don't you know we have people just begging to be locked up so they can partake of the sheriff's wife's cooking? Your brother is eating just fine, don't you worry none."

"Well, we brought it for him, so can we give it to him?" asked Big John.

"Sure. Take it on back. You aren't armed, are you?" he said laughing.

Ten minutes later Bobby and Big John were back in the office.

"You done already?" Casey asked them.

"He isn't in a talkative mood," said Bobby.

"Casey, we were wondering if you know where Fat Joe is? Have you guys checked him out regarding mama's murder?" Big John asked.

"We're asking around. The sheriff has an APB on him. We wanna know where he was the night your mama got killed. We figure it's a little suspicious he shows up and then your mama is killed. We'll let you know if we find out anything," Casey answered.

"Thanks," Big John said, as he and Bobby started walking out the door.

"Just one thing, though, Bobby," Casey said.

Bobby turned back, looked at him, and asked, "What's that?"

"So far, you're still the only one without a solid alibi."

As they were driving back to Big John's house, Bobby

said, "I didn't do it. I want you to know I could never hurt mom."

"I know, Bobby," Big John replied. "Never thought you did."

"Tom read mom's Will. I was there when he found it."

Big John was quiet for a moment. "Did you read it, too?" he asked Bobby.

"Some of it. I don't understand all that legal stuff. Tom was pissed off, though, when he read it. He said we had to wait years before we got any money."

"He had to wait six years. Mom wrote it so we would get a nice chunk when we hit thirty."

"How do you know?" Bobby asked him.

"Mom told me. We each were supposed to get two hundred and fifty thousand when we turned thirty."

"Then what?"

"Another two-fifty when we hit fifty and the balance when mom died."

"So, what happens now? Do we get it all now?" Bobby asked.

"I don't know. I guess we'll have to wait until David tells us," he answered.

"Tom won't get any, will he?" Bobby asked.

"Why wouldn't he get any?"

"I heard that you can't profit from trying to kill someone while you are in jail. For sure, he's gonna wind up in prison for what he did."

"So, if that's true, it means you and I will split it," said Big John.

Thirty

At approximately 11:30 p.m., the Monday following Melissa's death, a St. Louis police officer pulled Joe Johnson over. A sobriety test, given by the side of the road, indicated that he was drunk. He put Joe in the back seat of his squad car and drove him to the police station.

"This guy is wanted for questioning down in Hollister," the booking sergeant told the officer, after checking Joe's record. "I'll give 'em a call down there and let them know we got 'em."

Tom's and Hook's arraignment had been that morning and they were sitting in the Taney County Jail in Forsyth. Both men had pled not guilty. The judge had denied bail and they would be staying in the county jail until their trials.

Now, Joe was sitting in the same jail cell in Hollister, where his son, Tom, had spent the past few days.

Sheriff Berkson had used every tactic he knew to get Joe to confess to Melissa's murder. Unless he could prove that Joe was in the area on the night Melissa was killed, he was going to have to let him go. He had forty-eight hours and time was moving fast. Fat Joe kept silent until the sheriff asked him if Tom had hired him to murder his mother.

Joe laughed. "That boy ain't got no money. You're barking up the wrong tree, sheriff. I didn't have anything to do with it."

"How do you know he hasn't got any money?" the sheriff asked.

"'Cause I conned him out of every penny he had. His mama had just give'd him some money and I talked him right out of it. Gave him a hard-luck story and he fell for it. He's not real sharp, that one. Told me he'd be rich someday, but he'd be an old man before that happened."

"How do I know he didn't pay you that money to kill his mama? You hated her. I figure you might have done it for nothing," the sheriff said.

"No way you're gonna pin that on me. No, sir. I didn't kill that bitch."

"Watch your mouth, Joe. Melissa was a fine lady and you need to respect the dead."

"Probably, it was that boy, looking to get rich," said Joe.

"That boy you talking about, Joe. Well, he's sitting in county right now. We arrested him for attempted murder, not murder. He'll never be rich no matter how old he gets," the sheriff said.

"No shit?" said Joe. "He sure didn't seem to me like he'd have the guts for that."

"He hired someone to do it for him. And, I figure he hired you to do the job when the first try failed."

"Weren't me. I was nowhere around here. I left town the day after I stopped by and met Tom. No, sir. It wasn't me"

"Then you better tell me where you were that Tuesday night or you'll be sitting in here for a long time."

"Joplin. Call the sheriff in Joplin. I didn't tell you right off because I'm wanted there."

"For what?"

"That night you talking about. I'm pretty sure that's the same night I got into a scuffle with a cop and took off. There's a warrant out for my arrest for hitting him. I guess I'd rather face the music in Joplin than stick around here and be charged with a murder I didn't do. Check it out."

"I plan to, Joe. What time did all this go down?"

"I'm not sure. I was pretty shit-faced, but it was probably around eleven or twelve o'clock."

Sheriff Berkson and Casey were having a cup of coffee at Minnie's Diner.

"Man, that pie looks good," said the sheriff.

"It's fantastic. Minnie makes the best pie in the whole state of Missouri," said Casey as he took another bite of his apple pie.

"Hey, boy, watch your mouth. She's good, but nobody makes a pie like Sarah."

"Sorry. Wasn't thinking. Your wife's pie is the best. Just thinking about her pumpkin pie makes me wish it were Thanksgiving all over again."

"We're back to square one," said the sheriff. "We need to

start interviewing everyone again. I thought Fat Joe would be the one, but his alibi held up. Let's bring in both the sons again for a little talk,"

"I'll take care of it," said Casey.

"Bring in Big John's wife, too. I want to talk to her again. See if we can get search warrants for both their places. The judge probably won't issue them, but maybe we'll luck out this time. We probably won't find anything, but it never hurts to take a look."

"Will do. They aren't married, though," said Casey.

"Who isn't married?" the sheriff asked.

"Big Joe and Cynthia. Not married, just living together."

The sheriff looked at his phone, which was vibrating on the table. "Looks like there's a fire," he said.

"Where?" asked Casey.

"Out on Harper Lane."

The trailer burned fast. The fire department, knowing they couldn't save it, concentrated on wetting down the dry grass and brush in the back. Although, the weather was cool, it hadn't rained for a while and they didn't want to chance a fire starting in the woods.

Big John drove up just as the firemen were putting the hoses away. He walked over to the fire chief and said, "Thank god this didn't happen when my mom was still living here. This would have killed her."

Sheriff Berkson watched the fire trucks pull away. Well, he thought, if there was any evidence left in there, it's gone now.

"Sorry, Big John."

"Thanks, sheriff. Mom loved this place. She lived here for almost twenty-eight years. She didn't have much, but she didn't mind. The only thing that meant anything to her was that old grandfather's clock she got when grandpa died."

"Well, it's too hot to look around now, but maybe there's a few things left that you can salvage," the sheriff commented.

"Not much I'd want. Except, maybe that old clock," replied Big John.

Thirty-One

Immediately after Bobby walked into his apartment, there was a knock on his door. He opened it to see Casey standing there, hat in hand. Casey asked if he could talk to him for a few minutes and Bobby motioned to him to come on in. As Casey walked into the living room, he noticed an old grandfather clock standing in the corner of the room.

"Nice clock," he said. "You had that long?"

"It was my grandpa's," he told Casey. "It's probably the only thing of value that mama had in the house. I brought it over here right after Tom got locked up. I didn't want it staying there in an empty house."

"Bobby," Casey said, "You do know your mama's trailer just burned down, don't you?"

"What are you talking about? Oh, my god. I've got to call Big John and let him know."

"He knows," Casey told him. "He drove out there right after the fire department got the call. I figured he would have let you know."

"I was fishing. I stopped down at the marina and threw a line in. Mostly, I just sat there and stared at the water. God, Casey, what's happening? First, mama gets shot at, then smothered, Tom's in jail, and now her trailer is gone. Everything is falling apart." Casey watched as Bobby had a meltdown. He started sobbing, excused himself, and went to the bathroom. Casey heard him blow his nose before he came back out.

"Sorry, Casey. I just can't believe she's gone. And, this thing with Tom. He had to be drunk when he talked Hook into shooting mama. None of this makes any sense."

"Can you tell me why Big John didn't call you and tell you about the fire?"

"How should I know? I left my phone in my truck while I was fishing. I didn't check it for calls. He probably called me and I just missed the call."

"Okay. I'm out of here. By the way, the sheriff wants to talk to you again. Can you stop by sometime tomorrow?"

"Sure. I'll stop by over my lunch hour if that's good for him."

"I'll tell him you're coming in," said Casey. "One more thing, Bobby."

"What's that?"

"We'd like your permission to search your house. You can say no, but we'll just get a warrant."

"I haven't got anything to hide. Go ahead."

"How about we do it tomorrow?" Casey replied.

"Do I need to be here? With all that's going on, I don't want to miss any more work than I have to."

"No. We won't need you here," replied Casey.

"You need to answer your phone when I call you,

Bobby," shouted Big John. "I've been trying to call you for hours."

"I know about the fire if that's why you're calling. Casey stopped over and told me. My god, Big John, what else can go wrong? I'm at the point where I'm afraid to get up in the morning, not knowing what's gonna happen next."

"The sheriff wants to talk to me again," Big John said. "I don't know what else he thinks I can tell him."

"Ya, I'm going in at noon to talk to him. They're searching my apartment tomorrow, too. Grasping at straws, if you ask me. They sure aren't going to find anything here," Bobby responded.

"They got a search warrant, Bobby?"

"No. Casey said if I didn't let them in, they would get one."

"Call it off. We're making it too easy for them. You tell them if they want to search your place, you want to see a warrant. They won't get one. They don't have cause and no judge is going to issue a warrant."

"Isn't that gonna make them mad?" Bobby asked.

"Who cares? Just call the sheriff and tell him you've changed your mind. I'm sure not gonna let them into my house without one."

Big John met with the sheriff a little after nine the next morning. "So, Big John, tell me," the sheriff said, "Where were you when the fire started?"

Big John's head jerked up and he looked at the sheriff with a shocked expression. "What the hell, Cowboy? I was working. You know that."

"Seems to me you got to that fire real quick."

"Well, seeing as how I work for Pete and he's a volunteer, it's a wonder I didn't show up at the house before you did. When he said the fire was on Harper Lane, I had a bad feeling and decided I should go check it out. What's this about, anyway?" Big John asked. "What am I doing here?"

"Just wondering, that's all. I doubt we'll ever know how that fire started. It's a good thing Bobby got that old clock out of there, though."

"What clock?" asked Big John, confused.

"Your grandpa's old clock. It must have been hard for him to move that big thing all by himself."

"I guess," Big John mumbled.

"When you called Bobby, the night your mama was murdered, did you tell him she had been smothered?"

"I told you, sheriff. When I called him, I didn't know how she had died."

"Well," the sheriff continued, "Don't you think it's a little strange he knew that when he showed up?"

"Haven't really thought about it," Big John answered.

"What time did you go to bed that night?" the sheriff said, changing the subject.

"I think it was around ten. That's our usual time, so I guess it was ten," Big John said.

"Were you home all night?" asked the sheriff.

"I guess," said Big John.

"You guess?"

"I was home all night, alright?"

"You sure?" asked the sheriff.

"Sheriff, I left work and went straight home. I did not pass go and I did not collect $300.00."

"This a joke to you, Big John?"

"This whole conversation is a joke," he replied.

"It's $200.00," said the sheriff.

"What?"

"You collect $200.00, not $300.00," the sheriff told him.

"Seriously?"

"Well, I guess we're done for now. Don't leave town, though."

As Big John started walking towards the door, the sheriff's said, "The coroner thinks he might have been wrong about the time of death. It looks like she might have been murdered earlier than he thought."

Big John stopped walking for a second, then, without another word, left the building.

A couple of hours later, the sheriff was putting Bobby

through the same routine. "Why'd you call off the search, Bobby?" he asked. "You got something to hide?"

"Big John told me you needed a search warrant. He said I didn't need to let you in there snooping around for no good reason."

"Maybe, I've got a reason. Maybe you should stop listening to your big brother and start to cooperate. Where were you when the fire started?"

"What? I was working. I didn't even know about the fire until Casey stopped by and told me. I didn't have anything to do with that fire," Bobby said.

"We found a lighter in your truck. What do you need a lighter for?" asked the sheriff.

"What were you doing looking in my truck? You have no right."

"Sure, I do. I'm the sheriff. So, tell me, Bobby, how did you know your mother had been smothered?"

"Big John. Tom told him when he called him and then he told me. I figure that's what happened. Tom had to tell Big John."

"Big John says he didn't know when he called you," replied the sheriff.

"Well, he must have forgot."

"Did you work that day?" the sheriff asked.

"All day."

"What did you do after work?"

"I already told you. I did a little grocery shopping, went home, put the groceries away, and had a beer with a neighbor. I didn't go out and I was in bed early."

"You didn't leave your place after six-thirty?"

"That's right."

"The coroner thinks now that he got the time of death wrong. Your mom might have been murdered earlier than nine-thirty."

Bobby gave him a puzzled look. "Sheriff, the time of death doesn't change the fact that someone killed my mom. It wasn't me. If she was killed at six-thirty or eleven-thirty or any time in between, it makes no difference. She's dead and the time of death isn't going to change the fact that I've lost my mother. Why don't you quit looking at Big John and me and start doing your job?"

Two down, one to go, the sheriff thought as Bobby walked out of the police station. Cynthia was due to come in around four. He decided to go over to Minnie's Diner for some lunch.

Thirty-two

Sheriff Berkson and Casey were at their desks when Cynthia walked through the door to their office. They both stared as she walked towards them. She was wearing a halter-top that left little to the imagination and if her shorts had been any shorter, they could have passed for a belt. The look on her face told the sheriff she was more than ready for whatever he planned to throw at her.

"Hello, there, Cynthia. I just have a couple of questions. Have a seat."

"Well, hello to you, too. Sheriff," she said, with a smile that could make your knees weak.

"Casey, you want to get Cynthia something to drink?"

He looked over at Casey, who was still staring at Cynthia's boobs. "Casey," he yelled.

"Sorry, sheriff. What did you say?" Casey asked.

"Would you get Cynthia something to drink? What would you like, darlin'? A Coke or Pepsi?"

"Water is just fine," she replied with a smile. "I'm particular about what I put in my body. I never drink soda."

"Casey, get Cynthia a water."

"Yes, sir," Casey said, tripping over his own feet as he got up and came around his desk. "You want anything, sheriff?"

"Just get her a bottle of water," the sheriff said, trying

not to laugh.

"What can I do for you, sheriff? You sure do look handsome today."

"Why, thank you. So, let's get going so we can get you out of here. Would you be so kind as to tell us everything you remember about the night Melissa was murdered?"

"I don't know much. Big John and I ate dinner, watched a little TV, and went to bed."

"What time did you turn in?" the sheriff inquired.

"Around ten. We always go to bed at ten during the week," she answered.

"What time did the phone ring?"

"I didn't hear the phone. I took a sleeping pill and that knocked me out. I do remember Big John saying something and then he got out of bed. I guess that's when he got the phone call from Tom."

"So, you don't know what time he left the house?"

"I have no idea. He told me it was around one o'clock, but I don't know for myself."

"So, you slept all night?"

"Like a log."

"Big John could have gotten out of bed any number of times and you wouldn't know it?"

"I guess. But he would have told me. He tells me everything," she answered.

I just bet he does, thought the sheriff. "Cynthia, do you

know if Bobby and Melissa were getting along?"

"As far as I know, they were. Bobby never seems to stir the waters. Tom could set her off. I think he enjoyed it. But, Bobby – no."

"What about Big John? Was he getting along with his mom?"

"Seriously, sheriff? Big John adored his mother. It just about killed her when he finally moved out, even though she had been pushing all the boys to get their own places. It was a huge adjustment for him, too. They were really close. I really can't see either one of them hurting her. Tom is another story. He has a lot of growing up to do and when she came into that money, he thought she should spread the wealth with him."

"So, no real serious problems with any of them, as far as you know?"

"Nothing serious."

"Where were you when the fire started?"

"Not up on Harper Lane, that's for sure. Believe me, sheriff, when I light a fire, I make sure I put it out."

"I just bet you do," the sheriff said laughing. "How did you and Melissa get along?"

"I didn't like her, but I didn't kill her. We didn't have much to do with each other. She never asked me over for a meal or anything and we never asked her to go out to dinner with us. Big John and I talked about having her over, now that he has his own house, but we never got around to it. Maybe, I didn't take the time to know her. I probably should have made more of an effort, for Big John's sake. It's too late now."

"I guess that's it. Thanks for your time," the sheriff said.

"What is going to happen to Tom?" Cynthia asked as she got up to leave.

"He'll sit in county until he either takes a plea bargain or goes to trial. He'd be better off just confessing. A guilty verdict usually means more time than a plea bargain. Big John should go see him and tell him."

"Why can't he get out until his trial? I thought you could get out on bail."

"Not in this case. Judge is afraid he'll run. He'll be sitting there for a while. Did he get an attorney yet?" the sheriff asked her.

"Big John is working on getting him one, but we don't have the money to pay him. He'll probably wind up with a court-appointed one," she answered.

"What a shame. All that money sitting there and Tom can't even hire an attorney."

Cynthia wiggled her hips all the way to the front door and left. The sheriff looked over at Casey and said, "You can put your eyes back in your head now."

"I think I need a shower," Casey replied.

Thirty-three

Half the town showed up for Melissa's funeral, giving their condolences and support to the boys. The judge allowed Tom to attend the funeral service, but that was the extent of his short-lived freedom. Now, he was back in Forsyth County Jail, sitting in his cell.

Mary Ellen had driven down from Paw Paw and had spent the night with Big John and Cynthia. She had been tired when she arrived and they hadn't talked much before she went to bed.

The funeral service was over and people were leaving the cemetery. Bobby asked Mary Ellen if she wanted to join them for lunch and she said she'd be glad to, adding that she would follow them in her car to the restaurant.

As soon as the waitress had taken their order, Mary Ellen started asking questions. "I don't get it," she said to Big John. "You mean to tell me that Tom hired this guy, Hook, to shoot your mom? Why would he do that?"

"For the money, of course. He didn't want to wait six years to see any of her money. He figured if he got rid of her, he would get it his share right away," Big John told her.

"If he was hunting with you guys in Texas, how did he get caught? This whole thing sounds so confusing to me."

"Tom hired this guy Hook to shoot her. Hook had a little too much to drink and the sheriff picked him up for public intoxication. He started mumbling a bunch of nonsense and mentioned mom's name a few times. After the sheriff questioned him for a few hours, he confessed to what he had done and said it was all Tom's idea. He was mad at Tom for not paying him the money he promised."

"I didn't even get a chance to talk to Tom. He looked so sad," Mary Ellen said.

"At least they let him come to mama's funeral," said Bobby.

"Big deal. They took him right back to County Jail, as soon as the funeral was over", said Big John.

"Who does the sheriff think killed Melissa?" asked Mary Ellen.

"He doesn't know who. Fat Joe was ruled out. He was in Joplin. Tom has an iron-clad alibi. Of course, it wasn't me or Bobby. Right now, the sheriff hasn't got a clue who it was. Just who it wasn't," said Big John

"Money does strange things to people. So, Cynthia, I see a ring on your finger. When do you two plan on getting hitched?" Mary Ellen inquired.

"We haven't set a date, yet. We're not in any hurry, are we honey?"

"I guess not," said Big John.

"I want to mention a few things to you boys before I leave," Mary Ellen said.

"You're not going home today, are you? You can stay

with us as long as you want," said Big John.

"No, I've got to get back. I'm driving as far as St. Louis when I leave here and then I'll head home in the morning. I was wondering if I could take the clock back with me. It's rightfully mine and, although I hate to put it this way, your mother did steal it from me."

"The clock's gone," said Bobby.

"What do you mean, it's gone?" Mary Ellen asked.

"It was burnt in the fire," Bobby answered. Big John gave him a surprised look and Bobby winked at him.

"What fire?" asked Mary Ellen.

"The fire that burnt mama's trailer to the ground," Bobby told her.

"Her trailer's gone?" Mary Ellen exclaimed. "My, god, does it ever end with this family."

"I guess we've had a streak of bad luck lately," said Big John.

"You think?" Bobby laughed. "Could it get any worse?"

"I need to go over something with you," Mary Ellen told them. "You know you are my only living relatives. I guess Tom is out of the picture now, with him being in jail and all. Well, maybe he isn't. It all depends on when I die."

"Oh, Aunt Mary Ellen, don't talk like that. It will be a long time before that's going to happen."

"Well, what I want to mention is that... well, you know... what I'm trying to say is that you boys are all I have now," she said, tears swelling in her eyes. "I'm a wealthy woman. You know that. Even with the settlement that Peter got in our divorce, I have more than I'll ever need. I was going to leave everything to you three boys. But, with what's happened with Tom, trying to have your mom killed and all – well, I think I will leave most of it to you two."

"You and Peter got divorced?" Bobby said. "When did that happen?"

"Didn't your mama tell you boys anything?" Mary Ellen asked.

"Mary Ellen, please. We don't want your money. We have more than enough of our own," said Bobby.

"No, I've made up my mind. There are a few charities that I plan on leaving some money to, but the rest will go to you two."

"Well, Auntie, we just hope that's gonna be a long time from now."

"Of course," Mary Ellen added, "That's how it is today. I'm still a young woman. I just might get married again and then, of course, my new husband would get it all."

Bobby watched as Big John's smile disappeared.

"Food's here. Let's enjoy our meal," said Mary Ellen.

A couple of hours later, Bobby, Big John, and Cynthia were sitting in front of David Branson's desk, waiting for him to speak. He was concentrating on the papers in front of him and had barely said a word since they had arrived. Finally, he looked up and gave them a weak smile.

"It's pretty cut and dried," said David. "She wanted all her assets to be split evenly among you three boys upon her death."

"What about Tom? Does he still get a share?" asked Bobby.

"I'm pretty sure the answer to that is no. The law states that you can't profit from a crime. The fact that he and Hook conspired to kill your mom pretty much takes him out of the picture. For now, his share will go into a trust. If he is convicted, he receives nothing and his share will be split between you two.

"That doesn't seem fair to me," Bobby said.

"You know what, Bobby, life isn't fair. I don't think it's fair that your mom is gone, either. Shit happens and we have to learn to live with it."

"What are we looking at? Moneywise, I mean," asked Big John.

"Your mom was looking at a few different properties to buy. She had also talked to me about investing in the market and buying some equities. Fortunately, for you, she didn't get around to any of that, so there is nothing to liquidate. It's all cash money."

David stopped talking for a few seconds. He looked up at Melissa's two sons. "You two and Tom were all she talked about. You were her life, you know. I want you to know that I feel privileged to have known her. She was a good woman. I'm sorry I never told her, but I loved her. I can only hope she knew," he told them.

Big John looked at him and asked, "Whatever. How much?"

David looked at him in disgust and answered him. "As of this minute, the entire estate is worth $7,876,221.68. That changes every hour or so due to the interest."

"So, our share will be what, as of this minute?" asked Bobby.

"First, we have to file and pay whatever is due to the IRS for the money Melissa inherited from her father. She was told that the amount she was receiving would be after taxes, but that wasn't quite the case. We have to work that out first. Then, we'll have to file and pay the taxes on the money you will receive. After all the taxes are paid, along with my fee and miscellaneous expenses, you will probably walk away with about three million each. That's assuming Tom is convicted. If not, then it's a three-way split."

"What's left after we pay our taxes?" Big John asked.

"That's tax-free to you. The estate is paying the taxes."

"How much are your fees?" Bobby asked David.

"Roughly, one hundred fifty thousand," David told him. "You will be provided with a list of all of the expenses as we go along."

"How much can we get now? I'd like to get an attorney for Tom and so far, all of them want to be paid a retainer up front," said Big John.

"Give me a week or so. There's some work to do. I need to get copies of her death certificate. I figure I can easily send you all a check for around one hundred thousand by then."

"All the bills for the funeral expenses are coming to you. I told them that you would be paying for everything out of the estate."

"That's fine," David replied. "That's it. Any questions before we wrap this up?"

"Ya, I got one," said Bobby. "Was my mother any good in bed?"

"What the hell is wrong with you?" David yelled. "You just put your mother in the grave a few hours ago and now you sit here and disrespect her like that? Let me tell you something, you smart-ass. Your mother had more class in her little finger than you do in your whole body. You're a pig. Now, get the hell out of my office."

After they left David's office, Bobby and Big John decided to go have a beer at Waxy's,

"What the hell got into you?" Big John asked Bobby. "What were you thinking, asking him a question like that?"

"It just slipped out. I sat there looking at him, thinking

about how he was profiting off mom dying and I started to get pissed."

"You get pissed, so you ask him a question like that? We're all profiting off mom's death, Bobby."

"Not Tom," said Bobby.

"Maybe - maybe not. He sure as hell tried. Whatever. I don't care right now.

"Don't get me wrong. I don't want to see Tom wind up in prison, but that extra money of his would be nice."

"I figured we would get more. I forgot about all those damn taxes," said Big John.

"Fucking government," said Bobby.

Thirty-four

"Why are you just now coming forward with this information?" Sheriff Berkson asked. "Melissa was murdered over a week ago."

"I was out of town. I just found out about it yesterday, when I got back home," the woman told him.

"Didn't Deputy Funtelli question you after the murder?"

"I never talked to him. He came by at some time and left his card in my door. He wrote a little note on the back asking me to call. I didn't even see the card until this morning. I rarely use the front door."

Sylvia Toppers was a nice-looking woman with a good figure and a very nice tan. The sheriff guessed she was around thirty years old. She lived in a nice house about a half-mile down the road from Melissa's trailer. Word around town was that she had married a man with money and divorced him a year later. As far as the sheriff knew, she didn't have a job.

"How long have you lived out there now? Six or seven years?"

"Just about seven years," she answered.

"You sure have a nice tan. Been on vacation?"

"I just spent a week in Corpus Christi, visiting my sister," Sylvia told him.

"Walk me through this one more time. I want to be sure

I get the details right."

"Melissa was killed on the Tuesday before Thanksgiving, right?" Sylvia said.

"That's right."

"I drove by her place that night. It was around ten-thirty."

"Let me interrupt here, Sylvia. What were you doing out that time of night?" the sheriff said.

"I needed a few things for the trip, so I drove over to Walmart and did a little shopping."

"What kind of things?" the sheriff asked.

"Well, if you must know, I needed some Tampax. I also wanted to pick up a couple of gifts for my sister's kids, to take with me."

"You weren't out drinking?

"God, no. I rarely touch the stuff and I rarely go to bars," she told him.

"Go on," said the sheriff.

"Well, as I was driving by Melissa's on my way home, I saw Big John's truck parked by her house."

"On the side or in front?" the sheriff said.

"On the side."

"You sure it was Big John's? It must have been hard to see it if it was parked on the side."

"Oh, it was his, all right. There's no way you can miss that big-ass Ford. I saw that truck parked in front of that trailer every day since he bought it. Well, until he moved out. But it was his. No doubt in my mind."

"Sylvia, this is important. Would you be willing to swear in court and testify that his truck was parked there that night at around ten-thirty?"

"I would," she answered.

"You didn't happen to see anyone moving around or in the yard, did you?"

"Sorry. Can't help you there, Sheriff."

"You plan on staying in town? I really don't want you leaving," he told her.

"I just took a week's vacation. Christmas is coming and I plan to celebrate at my house this year. I sure can't afford to be running all over the country."

"I was wondering. Just what it is you do for a living?"

Sylvia chuckled a little. "Well, I did okay in the divorce. I get some alimony every month. Of course, if I ever married again, that would stop. I do some work on the internet for a medical group and make a little there. I'm certainly not well off, but I get by okay."

"You may have just solved my case for me. I guess it's time for me to talk to Big John."

Big John was sweating. Casey had stopped at the shop where he worked and asked him to take a little ride with him to the police station. Sheriff Berkson had been questioning him for the past forty-five minutes.

"She's lying. I wasn't there. How many times do I need to tell you?"

"You might as well just come clean, Big John. We have a witness who saw your truck there. You killed your mother. Why not just admit it and get this over with?"

"I didn't. I swear to god, I didn't do it."

"Well, I think you did. Cynthia has already told us that she took a sleeping pill that night. It would have been easy for you to slip out of bed, drive out to the trailer, smother her, and be back in bed by the time Tom found her and called you."

"I'm telling you. She's wrong."

"John Johnson, you are under arrest. You have the right to remain silent. If you do say anything, it can be used against you in a court of law. You have the right to have a lawyer present during any questioning. If you cannot afford a lawyer, one will be appointed for you, if you so desire."

"You're making a huge mistake, sheriff," Big John said, as Sheriff Berkson started to cuff him.

"Do you understand your rights?"

"I do. Will you call Cynthia and ask her to get me an attorney?"

"You can have a phone call. Why don't you call her?" the sheriff replied.

"Sheriff?"

"What?"

"I didn't do this. I'm innocent."

"That's what they all say, Big John. Everyone's always innocent."

Thirty-five

Tom refused a plea bargain. His trial took place the following spring. The jury found him guilty of attempted murder. He was sentenced to fifteen years in prison, with the possibility of parole in seven and a half years.

Six weeks after Tom's trial ended, Big John's began. He was convicted of murder and received a thirty-year sentence, with no chance of parole.

Both men are doing their time in Jefferson City State Prison. They see each other occasionally but rarely talk. Big John is convinced that Tom killed his mother. Tom is certain that Big John did it.

Hook was declared incompetent to stand trial. He spent sixty days in a state mental institution. He disappeared after his release and there is an outstanding warrant for his arrest. It is doubtful he will be found, though, as he is enjoying life on a small island in the Caribbean.

A week after Big John's trial was over, Bobby drove past the property where his mother's trailer had been. The weeds had taken over and the grass was brown. The blue picket fence was still there. One section had broken off and was lying on the ground. Bobby had a few seconds of remorse and a slight twinge of guilt as he drove by.

He stopped at a house a little down the road, parked his

car, got out, walked up to the front door, and knocked.

"It's been a long time, Bobby," Sylvia said as she answered the door.

"Too damn long," he replied, as he pulled her close to him and kissed her. "Damn, I've missed you."

"I've missed you, too."

Joyce Skoup walked into the living room, with a huge grin on her face.

"Hi, Bobby."

Bobby grinned back at her. "Hey, beautiful, I wondered where you were," he said.

"You know us old ladies, Bobby. Always in the bathroom," she laughed. "You got something for me?"

"I sure do. You are now the proud owner of a condominium on a beach in St. Petersburg, Florida," he told her, as he handed her a large envelope.

"Bless you. I'm gonna spend the rest of my days watching the waves roll in. What about you, Bobby? What are you planning to do with all that money?"

"Hell, between Hook and you two, half my money's already gone," Bobby said jokingly.

"I doubt that, but I figure I did okay for telling just one little lie," Joyce said.

"Tell me, Joyce. Does my truck make that much noise?"

"Hell, I don't know. I sleep like a log. I don't hear

anything once my head hits that pillow."

Joyce walked over to Bobby and kissed him on the cheek. "Thanks, again, Bobby. I've got some packing to do."

"See ya, Joyce," Bobby said.

"Back atcha," Joyce replied, as she walked out the door.

"Seriously, Bobby, what are you going to do now?" Sylvia asked him.

"Well, I'm thinking about taking a little trip up to Illinois."

"What are you going up there for?" Sylvia inquired.

"I want to find out if my Aunt Mary Ellen is a sound sleeper."

"For god's sake, Bobby, you just inherited almost eight million dollars. You got it all. You certainly don't need your aunt's money. Why risk it?"

"Because, my love, all is never enough."

"Then what, Bobby? There must be something you want to do, like travel or sail around the world. Or, move. Surely, you must want to get out of that apartment and move into some nice big house overlooking the lake," Sylvia said.

"Actually, I'm thinking about buying the biggest, fanciest, most expensive mobile home money can buy and setting it down right where I used to live."

"You got all that money and you want to buy a fucking trailer?" Sylvia yelled.

"Not a trailer," Bobby said, with a great big smile. "A

mobile home.

About the Author

Susan L. Pare was born in Idaho in 1939. Her father's job demanded that they frequently move and, by the age of ten, she had lived in Idaho, Montana, Colorado, Michigan, and finally Wisconsin. She lived in Wisconsin until she graduated from school.

Susan is the proud mother of three grown sons and two grandsons.

She worked as an accountant for most of her life. However, for the two years before she retired, she managed two Curves fitness facilities in Illinois.

She retired in 2002 and moved to Branson, MO. In 2012, she moved to Indiana to be closer to her family and lives there at present.

She enjoys a good laugh and loves dumb jokes. Reading has always been one of her passions and she still reads a couple of books a week. She started designing websites in 2003 and continues to maintain them in her spare time.

For most of her life, she has written short stories and poems for amusement. She wrote *Blueberries and Bears and My Brother's Shoes*, a book about growing up in the forties and fifties. After self-publishing it and giving it to friends and family to read, they encouraged her to get serious about her writing.

Blueberries and Bears and My Brother's Shoes is being edited to make it more reader-friendly and should be ready for release in early 2016.

Follow her on her website: www.susanlpare.com.

www.ingramcontent.com/pod-product-compliance
Lightning Source LLC
Chambersburg PA
CBHW070844120626
46556CB00002B/875